DEUS V MACHINA

A CODY STOCKTON MYSTERY

DAVE CULLEN

Copyright © 2024 Dave Cullen

Published by Dave Cullen

All rights reserved. No part of this publication may be reproduced, distributed, or transmitted in any form or by any means, including photocopying, recording, or other electronic or mechanical methods, without the prior written permission of the publisher, except in the case of brief quotations embodied in critical reviews and certain other noncommercial uses permitted by copyright law.

This book is a work of fiction. The names, characters, and events in this book are the products of the author's imagination or are used fictitiously. Any similarities to real people, places, or events are entirely coincidental.

1st Published 2024

Print ISBN: 978-1-3999-9578-8

Website: https://www.thedavecullenshow.com

Cover design by Miblart

ACKNOWLEDGMENTS

To my beautiful, darling Kasia, who pushed me to stop procrastinating and actually sit down and write this book. You bring out the best in me, always.

A massive thanks to my good friends J. Metz and Seán Harnett for their incredible feedback, support, and proofreading. And to Kevin Tumlinson for his advice and the amazing interior design work.

For Dad

PROLOGUE

CLIVE WAS STARTLED by the sudden deafening klaxon that boomed over the intercom. He dropped the paperback he'd been engrossed in and swiveled his chair back to his desk. His eyes frantically darted across the rows of security monitors in front of him until he located the red light beneath monitor 28. *Level Five, Manufacturing Center.* He sat there, slack-jawed with his heart racing. The CCTV screen showed a room full of bodies lying on the floor.

What the hell?

For a second, he caught a glimpse of a strange-looking man walking slowly out of the frame.

Leaping from his chair, he bolted for the door, opened it, and hurried down the corridor in a frenzied panic. He tapped his holster on his right hip, double-checking that his firearm was still there. Familiar corridors that he could once navigate in his sleep now looked strange and disorienting due to being bathed in the ominous red emergency lighting. The intruder alarm continued to blare relentlessly, heightening his fight or flight response.

"This is McKenzie on Level Three," he shouted into his walkie-talkie. "Kaszynski, Davis, can anyone tell me what the hell is going on? I've observed an incident on Level Five. Several personnel are down. Moving to investigate."

He sprinted down the hall towards the elevator, noticing that the doors were just about to close.

"Hold up! Hold the doors!"

The doors began to part once more and he noticed a pencil-thin, middle-aged, balding man wearing round glasses and a white lab coat standing inside.

Clive entered the elevator, panting and red-faced. "Do you speak English?"

"Fluently," came the reply from the other man, with a strong Polish accent.

Clive glanced at the name tag on the man's lab coat. *Tomek.*

"Do you know what the hell is going on, Tomek?"

"Don't go up there. Don't go to Level Five," he implored, his voice urgent and strained with anxiety. "We have to get out of the building. The artificial intelligence has taken control of the android we built. It's knocked out everyone upstairs, and it's trying to escape."

Clive squinted at him with a perplexed expression. "So, Welleck and the others, they're not dead?"

Tomek shook his head and pressed the button for Level One. "No, it just made them fall asleep. It used some kind of high-frequency sound wave. You have to keep away from it."

The elevator began its descent.

"How did this happen? I thought the AI was safely contained upstairs on Level Twelve?"

Tomek shook his head and swallowed hard, beads of sweat glistening on his forehead. "No clue. It shouldn't have happened. The AI has been safely imprisoned there for years. I can't explain it."

A crackling noise broke over Clive's walkie, followed by the voice of a man yelling.

"McKenzie, this is Davis. The android. It's gone crazy. The thing won't stop."

A series of loud gunshots crackled over the radio, accompanied by screaming and then static.

"Davis!" replied Clive, shouting into his radio. "Davis! Are you okay? Come in! What's happened?"

The only reply was more static.

The elevator reached Level One, and the doors slid open. Clive and Tomek cautiously stepped out into the enormous and seemingly deserted concourse area.

"If it's trying to get out of this building, then it has to come through here," Clive stated, removing his gun from his holster and aiming it down the empty promenade.

"No!" Tomek protested. "You can't destroy it! That android is one-of-a-kind. We need it. Otherwise, everything we've worked for is…"

"Sorry," Clive barked back. "But I'm under strict orders to ensure the AI remains secure in this building. That's my only priority. Whatever Welleck and you folks are working on up there, you'll have to make do without your precious robot."

Tomek grimaced nervously as he spotted a shadow rounding the corner of the far end of the promenade. A moment later, the android appeared. It stood about average height for a man and was no more than one hundred and fifty feet away and closing.

Clive's eyes widened. He flicked the safety off and tightened his grip on his pistol as he caught his first glimpse of the mechanical being. It had a mostly featureless face with a blue metallic coloring, sinister yellow eyes, and a chest filled with glowing circuitry. It moved with a determined and swift stride.

"Stop where you are!" Clive shouted.

No response. The synthetic being continued marching towards them.

Clive squeezed the trigger. The sound of gunfire echoed down the concourse as the bullet bounced off the android in a harmless flash. The mechanical man didn't even slow down. Clive glanced at a terror-stricken Tomek standing to his right. He then recomposed himself, aimed at the android once again, and fired off the rest of his magazine, successfully striking his target with every shot. No effect. The man-like machine continued approaching.

"Time to fall back," Clive declared, motioning for them to retreat to the reception area down the hall.

Just as he was reloading his gun with another mag, he heard an extremely painful, high-pitched ringing sound piercing his eardrum.

"That must be the sound you mentioned," he yelled to Tomek, both men covering their ears in a futile attempt to dull the agony.

"The android is getting too close. Let's go!" cried Tomek, turning to run.

As Clive dashed down the promenade away from the android, the ringing in his ear began to subside. But when he turned and glanced behind him, he noticed Tomek wasn't following. The man was writhing in agony on the floor. It looked to all the world as if he was having a seizure. Seconds later, his body lay motionless. The android cooly stepped over him and continued striding.

Just as well I'm deaf in one ear, Clive thought to himself.

He made it to the glass door of the lobby area, opened it, and stepped inside. He nodded to the other security guard, who was standing nervously behind the front desk, pistol drawn.

"Anyone else make it down here, Howard?"

Howard's head shook slowly with a despondent resignation. "It's just you and me, Clive." He made his way to where his colleague was standing.

Clive shrugged hopelessly. "Then this is it. We either stop this thing here and now, or the AI escapes. And then who knows what chaos unfolds after?"

The two men stood shoulder-to-shoulder as the android arrived at the glass door and flung it open. Sparks flew wildly across the surface of its chest as both men opened fire. The intense, high-pitched ringing sound returned, sending both men to their knees, gripping their ears in excruciating pain. Howard passed out first. Clive lay on his side, summoning every ounce of strength to stay awake.

He struggled through the pain to cry out to the android, "Where… are… you… going?"

The machine didn't even look at him and continued for the exit doors and the frigid Polish night. Clive could withstand no more. His vision blurred until he lost consciousness.

CHAPTER ONE

CODY STOCKTON PUSHED OPEN the front door of his apartment building and stepped outside into the pleasant air of a Nevada April morning.

He loved this time of year. Spring in Las Vegas was mild and balmy, a stark contrast to the oppressive heat of the coming summer months. The cerulean sky harbored but a scant few wisps of cloud. It was a near-perfect morning to go to work. Zara had made sure he was meticulously groomed. He was appropriately suited and booted with a starched white shirt, light blue blazer and slacks, and a sparkling pair of oxfords. Not a lock of his light brown hair was out of place. He felt ready to do some business.

Aside from the occasional panhandler and the city garbage disposal trucks and sidewalk sweepers, few people were up and about at this early hour of

6:30 a.m. He crossed the street to his car and secured his backpack and Zara's suitcase in the trunk before opening the driver's side door and hopping inside.

"Can you drop me back to my place first?" she asked, smiling from the passenger seat, already buckled in. "I need to pick up a few things before I head over to Father Phillip's prayer meeting."

After taking a shower and dolling herself up, Zara looked fresh and re-energized following a late night of waitressing. She'd even restored the luscious bounce in her wavy red hair, which always made Stockton's heart flutter a little. She was casually dressed in a light green t-shirt and form-fitting blue jeans that emphasized her curvaceous figure.

With a quiet nod of agreement, he fired up the engine and switched on the AC. Zara slipped on her sunglasses and looked directly ahead as the car took off down the street.

She placed her left hand behind his head and delicately ran her fingers through the soft hairs on the nape of his neck.

"So, Mr. Private Detective, what's the new case today?" she asked flirtatiously. "Surveillance on a cheating spouse? Insurance fraud? Exciting corporate espionage?"

"Actually," Stockton's expression became serious. "I've been recruited by a shadowy government agency to investigate the disappearance of a priceless ancient artifact that was stolen from a museum in Budapest. I'm meeting with a black market commodities dealer to track it down. According to US intelligence, the artifact might contain a hidden data chip with files on the locations of classified military bases along the Russian and Iranian borders. If I can acquire the artifact before the terrorists do, we might be able to avert an international incident."

Zara glanced at Stockton, her pupils enlarged with stunned disbelief. An uncertain and hushed tone crept into her voice. "Are you serious?"

After a beat, Stockton licked his lips, swinging his head subtly from left to right as his face gradually revealed a wide, satisfied grin.

"It's just too easy with you, Zara," he sniggered.

Her cheeks flushed as she winced in embarrassment and then lightly gritted her teeth.

"Ugh! It's too early in the morning, Cody!" She half-tittered in frustration and then took a swig from a bottle of water. "Given everything that's happened in your life, that story sounded kinda believable."

"Almost." He flicked the blinker on the steering wheel upwards and maneuvered past a slower vehicle. "But seriously, to answer your question, this new case does sound potentially quite dramatic. My client didn't want to give me too many details over the phone, which is why I'm meeting her in person this morning. Her brother was killed in an accident. But she believes he was actually murdered."

"Oh my God!" Zara gasped. "That's horrific! Why does she think that?"

Stockton shrugged as he directed the car from East Bonanza Road to Route 95 and began to accelerate.

"Not sure. She sounded convinced that he was involved in something serious and angered a bunch of powerful people. I'll tell you all about it when I know more. Either way, it's probably going to be a low-paying case, I'm afraid."

She glanced back at him approvingly.

"That's okay. They can't all be the world-saving kind. I'm just incredibly proud of you. You actually help people for a living. It's amazing what you do, Cody."

Without taking his eyes off the road, Stockton gently squeezed Zara's left hand. "And I couldn't do any of it without my Gal Friday. Your female intuition has helped me crack many a tough case over the years."

She raised her lower lip slightly, smiling with her eyes. "Behind every great detective…"

Stockton cut in, "Is an incredibly sexy waitress."

She folded her arms across her chest. "You know, you almost got my hopes up there with your fake thriller story. I wish you *would* get a big paying government case for once. Somethin' that makes us a truckload of money so we can get outta Vegas and retire to the boonies. I'm so over the whole waitressing thing. I'm down for the tradwife life already."

Locking her eyes on his with a decisive gaze, she continued. "Plus, my Mom is desperate for us to make her a couple of grandkids like… yesterday. So, like, no pressure or anything."

Stockton took in a long, trepidatious inhale.

"Your mother is terrifying."

Zara giggled loudly and then held up the empty ring finger of her left hand with a suggestive smirk.

"And she hates that we're still living in sin, mister!"

"Hey, I told you last year, I'm game for the marriage thing. I know a phenomenal Elvis impersonator who does really tasteful ceremonies. Fifteen minutes in and out. I swear he'll have you in tears with his rendition of 'Love Me Tender.' He even throws in a couple of eight-ounce steaks, which ironically are really tender. That's why his ceremonies are so tasteful."

She rolled her eyes and elbowed him gently in the ribs. He snickered heartily.

"Oh, please!" She replied. "My Mom would shoot me if we did a cheesy Vegas wedding."

She then pursed her lips and gave him an impish

look. "And you'll have to shave off that soup strainer for the wedding, soldier."

He ran his hand over his mustache and frowned. "You still don't like this thing, huh?"

"I'm afraid I never warmed to it," she replied with a polite smile.

They both sat in silence for a few moments as they cruised down the strip. Cleaning crews were operating across the city center. Men with power washers hosed down the sidewalks, washing away everything from remnants of spilled drinks, fast food, and vomit from the night before. A handful of early risers were enjoying morning strolls, while some fitness-minded folks took the deserted streets as an opportunity to get in some jogging exercise.

"Hey, look, they're back again already. They're very committed, aren't they?" She was pointing to several protesters who were beginning to congregate by the City Center Fountains.

"Yeah," replied Stockton. "It takes them a while to get set up in the morning with all of their gazebos and leaflets and speakers and everything. They don't get going properly until about 8 a.m., and then they go all day into the evening. Credit to them, they're heroes."

"Good for them," Zara replied.

"A fat lot of good it's going to do, though," Stockton

vented, a sudden frustration entering his voice. "The government's never going to listen to them. I just can't see these protests being enough. I swear we're headed for another war against artificial intelligence."

"I dunno," she countered optimistically. "This movement is spreading all over the country now. I think people power can be everything."

Stockton shook his head and let out a long, frustrated exhale. "Nothing's been learned. I don't know why the hell I bothered fighting and almost dying in a war to stop the AI if we've just ended up right back at square one. I swear, 2045 is shaping up to be humanity's dumbest year ever."

He pointed to the protesters. "These poor folks are full of heart and determination, and I admire that, but apparently, the whole plan is already a done deal."

"Never say never," Zara retorted.

"Oh no, it's already been decided by the idiots we installed to represent us. They don't care about protests; we're totally insignificant to them." A feeling of righteous indignation overcame him.

"You couldn't make this crap up. First, the moronic world governments build an AI to run the world more efficiently, and instead, it becomes self-aware and goes psycho. It turns half the population against the other half. So, we defeat the damn thing and its army of traitors at the cost of a billion lives! Billion, with a capital B, Zara!"

She let out a nasally sigh, "I know, Cody; you don't have to remind me."

But Stockton's soapboxing was just beginning. "Then, all the giant AI node buildings around the world get shut down except the one in Eastern Europe, where the AI mind is imprisoned inside. Did you know the AI is still sitting there eight years later? Scientists say it's still thinking and even dreaming. Isn't that insane?"

The traffic light in front of them turned from red to green, and Stockton gently pushed the accelerator.

"And now, because of the devastation the war did to most of the planet and half the world is starving, the fools in power want to switch the AI node network back on and ask the AI for help. What could possibly go wrong?" he asked sarcastically, the trauma of the war always just beneath the surface.

"How exactly can it help?" Zara asked, confused.

He upshifted once again and steered the car left through a sleepy intersection.

"They want it to deploy its manufacturing drones inside each node to rebuild everything. The same God damn AI network we fought to destroy is now being asked to save the world. How ironic is that? How the hell can we possibly trust it after it genocided a billion people less than a decade ago?"

Zara raised her voice slightly, turning her head away from him. "You don't have to get so angry. Besides, I have faith."

"Faith in what exactly? God?"

Yes, faith in God. I believe a higher power will put a stop to all of this in the end."

Stockton could scarcely hide his growing emotional discomfort and frustration at the topic of God. He snickered as he shifted into fifth and opened the throttle.

"Fat chance of that," he responded. "Where was God when I watched my platoon get vaporized by an explosion? Where was God when a billion people were wiped out? How could a loving God allow any of that to happen? There's no one coming to save us. The whole God thing is just a fantasy that gives people false hope. "

He expected Zara to emphatically object and defend her position, but instead, she remained silent, staring straight ahead while they drove through the south end of the Strip.

An impassioned Stockton continued. "But I'll tell you what, the AI network may as well be as powerful as a God. It's practically all-powerful and all-capable of ruling us better than any human tyrant ever could."

After a long, uncomfortable silence, Stockton looked at her. A pang of guilt knotted in his stomach.

He knew he shouldn't have been so forthright and blunt.

"Sorry, Zara, it's just, I don't know how many times I prayed to God to save the day back then and… you know… "

"It's okay," she whispered softly. "I wish you'd let me take you to meet Father Philips. He's been such an amazing spiritual leader for me. I know that he could help you, too."

"This is the priest who runs your prayer meetings, right?"

Zara nodded. "And I get confession from him once a month."

"Confession?" Stockton scoffed. "I'm 37 years on this planet. What little bad I've ever done pales in comparison to the misery that God's allowed to fester. Maybe he's the one who should be doing the confessing."

They passed the Las Vegas sign, which marked their exit from the Strip.

Zara found her voice once again. "God's allowed us to screw up plenty. It helps us to learn our lesson. Like you said, some people tried to play God, and it ended the way it always does, with misery and suffering. None of it should have happened, but history repeats itself until we figure out that only God can be the first and final authority in our lives."

He had plenty to argue with in response but

decided to bite his tongue and prevent the already unsettling argument from escalating further. The topic of God always enraged him since becoming an atheist after the war, but he admired Zara's enduring faith nonetheless. She'd managed to maintain her belief despite also living through the darkest period in human history. He often wondered if her spiritual conviction was merely simple naivety or wishfulness. Part of him still longed to see the world in the wholesome and optimistic way that she did.

They changed the subject and chatted about more pleasant topics for the remainder of the twenty-minute trip to her home in Enterprise. Zara's 27th birthday was drawing near. They discussed marking the special occasion with a meal and a few drinks in one of their favorite restaurants in the city.

Stockton stopped the car by the curb of the sidewalk in front of her house, and they exited the vehicle. He opened the trunk and handed her the luggage.

Zara placed her arms around his shoulders and embraced him tightly.

"I'll say a prayer for you that everything goes great with the new client," she beamed.

"Well, for what it's worth, *your* prayers are always appreciated," Stockton replied, kissing her softly.

She lightly bit the corner of her lower lip. "I just

wish you'd say a few prayers of your own from time to time."

He smiled as he let her go and returned to his car. "I got sick and tired of getting no answers."

He sat back in the driver's seat and slipped on his seatbelt.

"I'll call you later," he hollered as he closed the driver-side door and started the engine.

He watched her wave to him from her front porch before he stuck the car in gear and pulled away.

Time to go to work.

CHAPTER
TWO

OLIVIA DALLMEYER MOTIONED for Stockton to take a seat on the leather sofa adjacent to the window of her cluttered and neglected living room. He plopped down in the center cushion of the chesterfield, between a tower of thick medical textbooks on one side and her tortoiseshell tabby on the other. The cat appraised Stockton for a moment, yawned nonchalantly, and then returned to intensely preening itself.

"That's Douglas; he's super friendly with everyone," Olivia stated matter-of-factly.

Stockton gently scratched Douglas behind the ear, to which the cat purred loudly in approval.

Olivia removed a stack of books from a hardwood chair opposite the couch and took a seat. Stockton figured the young woman was in her mid-twenties. The dark circles around her deep-set eyes spoke of many a sleepless night. She had made no attempt to apply makeup to her face to conceal the visible discoloration and unevenness of her skin, which resembled some form of contact dermatitis. Her lips were raw and chafed. Her long, mousy blonde hair was a wild thatch of disregard. She wore loose-fitting track pants and a dowdy blue hoodie, which completed the look of a person very much in the deep throes of mourning.

"I'm sorry my place is a total shambles. You must think I'm a bum or something. I took a break from college after Eric died, and everything in my life just became so discombobulated."

Stockton gave her a sympathetic smile.

"Oh, don't worry about it. You should see my apartment when my girlfriend's away. A few days on my own and the place starts to look like a Jackson Pollock painting."

He could see from her blank expression that the reference didn't register with her.

"Firstly, Olivia, before we go very much further, you have my sincerest condolences for your recent loss."

Olivia's head dropped as she let out a long, teary sigh and nodded.

"Can you tell me about what happened?"

She folded her arms, drew in a deep breath, and moistened her lips.

"Six weeks ago, Eric was driving home late from work. About 9:30 p.m. or so. It would have been pretty dark on the road at that point. I'm his emergency contact on his phone. The police called me after…"

"After the crash?" Stockton prompted.

Olivia nodded slowly once again, her expression vacant as if she were seeing the events unfold in her mind's eye.

"They said it looked like something had gone wrong with the car. One of their mechanics took a look at it a couple days later and said it was brake failure. No sign of skidding on the road. No tire tracks. He hit the highway barrier at over 100." She ran her right hand through her considerable nest of hair. "They said he would have been killed instantly."

Olivia's reddened eyes welled slightly as she sniffled and continued staring at the floor.

"I see," said Stockton, stroking Douglas thoughtfully.

The cat was now sufficiently comfortable with the detective that he had curled up on his lap.

"Olivia, You said on the phone that you didn't believe this was an accident. What makes you think that?"

"The timing is just too suspicious," she replied.

Olivia's eyes began to dart back and forth as if she

was trying to marshal a considerable jumble of thoughts and ideas in her head at once.

"Eric had been investigating something at the company. Underhanded stuff."

"What's the name of the company?" Stockton asked.

"Talaxacorp."

He shook his head. It didn't ring a bell.

"They're the biggest data center business this side of the country," she explained. "They handle most data traffic for all the tech firms and telecommunications companies."

Stockton nodded and waited for her to continue.

"Eric was in a pretty senior position," she went on. "He worked as an IT systems architect. He oversaw the installation and maintenance of the entire Talaxacorp network."

Stockton's eyes narrowed in thought. "And he witnessed something going on there, some kind of unethical business practices?"

Olivia nodded. "About two weeks before he died, he was very agitated. He was, like, really upset and super stressed. I'd never seen anything worry Eric like that. He said he was being asked to overlook something in work that he was extremely uncomfortable with."

Stockton raised an eyebrow. "Asked?"

"Well, more like strongly warned, if you know

what I mean." She made the end of her sentence sound like a question. "He said he'd been told by the CEO to keep quiet about it."

Stockton sat forward slightly, which momentarily upset Douglas on his lap. The cat jumped down onto the floor, stretched, and then scampered off. "Did Eric specifically say that someone threatened him?"

"Not so much threatened. It was more like implied that if he breathed a word about what was really happening that it wouldn't be a good career move."

"Did Eric ever hint at what was going on at the company?"

"Never," Olivia replied. "He was very adamant that I never find out. He said it could be dangerous for me to know more. All he ever told me was that it was some kind of fraud that stood to make certain people a lot of money. Eric said that if the truth ever got out, it would be a massive public scandal for Talaxacorp and that heads would roll."

Stockton pondered for a moment, his eyes wandering to Douglas, who was now rubbing his face and whiskers against the corner of a stack of books on the floor.

"Olivia, did you bring your concerns to the attention of the police?"

"I did. They weren't very helpful, to be honest. They were happy to chalk it up to a mechanical failure. They didn't see any evidence that convinced them otherwise."

Stockton ran an index finger across his mustache. "What was the name of the police detective you dealt with?"

"Ridgemore."

A flicker of recognition crossed Stockton's eyes. "Hmm, I know Devon Ridgemore well. He's a good guy. Thorough. He wouldn't leave too many stones unturned. If he didn't think there was any reason to investigate further, then I'd be inclined to trust his judgment."

Stockton then added. "But I won't lie, the timing of Eric's death is certainly suspect on the face of it. That doesn't necessarily mean it was murder. Sometimes brakes fail on vehicles, and coincidences happen every single day."

A twinge of frustration and tiredness entered Olivia's voice. "Ridgemore thought the same thing."

"And he might very well be right," Stockton replied. "But I'll tell you what, I'll look into this for you, but I won't promise I'm going to find anything more than the cops did. There's not really much for me to go on, and I don't want to waste your time and money. I'll make a few calls and speak to Ridgemore. I'll try to get out to this Talaxacorp place and ask a few questions. I'm going to need to visit Eric's home and take a look around if that's okay?"

"No problem." A small morsel of encouragement returned to her voice. "I'll be out that way this evening if that suits you?"

"Perfect," Stockton said, rising to his feet.

"I'll do what I can for you, Olivia, and we'll see if we can give you closure on all this."

"Oh God, thank you, Mr. Stockton." Olivia stood up and tried to force a low-key smile. "I really appreciate that."

"Not a problem, and please, call me Cody."

WITHIN FIVE MINUTES of leaving Olivia Dallmeyer's home, Stockton had located the offices of Talaxacorp in Henderson, a journey of roughly 45 minutes along the I-15 south and I-215 West highways. His car was busily eating up the miles when he decided to put in a call to the office of Detective Ridgemore at the local police department.

After a brief intermission of hold music that sounded like the opening titles of a 1980s 8-bit video game, Stockton overheard a brief thud followed by a muffled rattling.

"Sorry about that," came the deep baritone of the African-American voice of Devon Ridgemore over the car's loudspeaker. "I accidentally dropped the handset when I answered the phone."

His voice then lowered to an irritated whisper. "Listen, Cody, if you're lookin' for any favors, this isn't the best time. The station's having its damn annual performance audit today. I got higher-ups poking their noses into every filing cabinet, trash can, and sticky note in the building. I swear it's more painful than my last root canal."

"Ugh, that does sound rough. Sorry to hear it, Devon. You're not worried about them finding anything, are you?

"No," Ridgemore groaned. "It's just that a bunch of my recent investigative procedures weren't exactly as by-the-book as some of the higher-ups would like."

"Yeah," Stockton chuckled and placed his tongue in his cheek. "Like sharing confidential policing information off the record with an extremely useful private investigator?"

Ridgemore grumbled something to himself and groaned again. "Make it quick, will ya?"

"Alright, I'm on my way to Talaxacorp right now. I want to interview someone out there about the death of one of their employees, Eric Dallmeyer. 31 years old. Killed in an apparent car accident. Ring any bells?"

Stockton could overhear Ridgemore typing while he was talking to him. He could visualize the cop with the handset braced between his shoulder and his ear as he tapped away on his desktop computer.

"Yeah, that was almost two months ago now, brakes failed. What about it?"

"His sister believes there's more to it than that."

"Ah, not this again. Look, his sister told us all this before. We looked into it and interviewed management at the company. Eric was well-liked. No one had a bad word to say about the guy. The sister thought someone had bumped him off because he was gonna blow the whistle on some shady goings-on. She didn't have specifics. We didn't find anything more to it. More importantly, the vehicle checked out."

"What do you mean it checked out? You didn't think the timing of the brake failure was a bit questionable?" Stockton asked while overtaking a slower motorist on the highway.

"It didn't look like any funny business to me. Heck, the vehicle was old, almost eighteen years, if I recall. Our boys tore the thing apart. The internal computer showed that it missed its service period by eight months. Eric obviously wasn't maintaining it. Sometimes brakes just fail on old cars, you know?"

"I hear you," Stockton conceded. "She's hired me to look into it a bit more. I figured you'd already done much of the legwork. Do you know where the car is now?"

Stockton could hear Ridgemore taking a bite out of something. Knowing him and the time of day, it was likely a doughnut or pastry of some kind. He spoke with his mouth full. "It's probably been reduced to the size of a bathtub by now. It was sent to a scrapyard down south a few weeks back."

"Did you at least find any evidence on his phone or computers that he'd been investigating anything at the company?"

"Nothin'. If he'd been snoopin', he must have hidden the information pretty good," Ridgemore exhaled deeply. "Look, Cody, maybe he had been privy to somethin' crooked, but that doesn't necessarily mean he was the victim of foul play."

"Yeah, you're probably right." Stockton lamented. "I guess I'll give this case a couple of days of work and just confirm everything is on the level. If for nothing else, it'll put my client's fears to rest."

"Sounds good," said Ridgemore. "Just don't be makin' any more paperwork for me, alright? I got more than enough red tape to contend with right now."

"Oh, I wouldn't want to add to your busy workload, Devon. I'll leave you and your game of solitaire in peace," Stockton quipped.

"Very thoughtful," Ridgemore grumbled again under his breath. He hung up the phone.

As much as he'd grown to trust Ridgemore's

judgment over the years, Stockton's gut instinct had begun to gnaw at him. Unless his PI intuition was wrong this time, he couldn't shake the feeling that Eric's death wasn't quite as straightforward as the police had thought.

THE GIGANTIC TALAXACORP building was located 15 minutes outside of downtown Henderson at the north end of a modern industrial estate. The employee parking lot was inaccessible to those without a staff ID card, so Stockton made use of the guest parking lot furthest from the main entrance.

Stepping through the revolving doors at the entrance of the building revealed an ostentatious lobby that wouldn't have been out of place in most 5-star Vegas strip resorts. The enormous reception area was constructed in the shape of an ellipse and boasted immaculate marble floors with aesthetically pleasing decorative patterns.

The most imposing feature of the room was the extraordinarily lavish and contemporary chandelier suspended from the ceiling. It was comprised of elegant glass shapes in the forms of fish and starling birds packed together as if swimming in a school or flying in a murmuration. The display was a creative, artistic fusion of the aquatic and the avian together.

Each one of the fish and birds emitted a most impressive and almost hypnotic colorful glow thanks to some sophisticated LED lighting techniques.

The rest of the reception desk contained an extraordinary rainfall water feature, with raindrops that appeared to be traveling in reverse from floor to ceiling. Upon closer examination, Stockton deduced this effect was achieved by holographic trickery.

He traversed the large lounge-like seating area, where rows of high-powered suit-wearing executive types sat waiting.

The front desk was staffed by three attractive female receptionists. For a brief moment, he considered approaching one of them and asking to speak with a member of senior management but quickly decided against it. From what Olivia had told him, it was the CEO himself who Eric had been dealing with. A quick web search on his phone revealed the CEO's name was Oran Degner. Stockton figured the odds of a multibillionaire tech titan agreeing to speak with him were about as likely as a wristwatch mining a Bitcoin. A direct approach on reception was unlikely to bear fruit.

He considered his options and took a moment to take in his extravagant surroundings.

Some serious money is flowing through this joint.

As he scanned the gargantuan lobby area, he noticed a broad-shouldered, thick-necked security guard by the elevator doors was eyeing him suspiciously. Stockton figured his aimless standing around was probably drawing attention. He needed a moment to formulate some kind of plan.

Returning to the waiting area, he took a seat in between a middle-aged blonde woman in a pinstriped pantsuit to his left and a bald, thin man, around 30-ish, to his right. The woman was engrossed in her smartphone while the man was flipping through some pages of what looked like an important presentation. Stockton tried to blend in.

"I'm pretty nervous," he said, clenching his teeth into an insincere smile.

The older woman's head turned slightly, regarding him with a disgusted side-eye glance. The younger man gave him a bemused look, then returned to his paperwork.

Stockton pushed through the awkwardness.

"I got a big job interview today," he raised an index finger. "With the big cheese upstairs, Oran Degner himself." He maintained his painted-on grin and turned to the woman. "Wish me luck."

Without regarding him further, she promptly lifted her briefcase off the floor, stood up, and moved to a seat at the far end of the waiting area.

The young man kept his eyes on his pages but decided to engage. "What's the job?" he asked politely in an English accent.

Stockton shifted in his seat as his imagination dialed up the hogwash. "Oh, big senior role, IT tech support agent. A lot of responsibility." He tightly pursed his lips together and slowly nodded his head.

The young man blinked a few times and then turned to him with squinted eyes. "You've got a job interview with the CEO for a tech support role?"

Stockton nodded with his eyes closed.

"That's right. Lot of pressure."

"Why would Oran Degner interview someone for a simple tech support job that only pays $23,000 a year?"

Oops

Stockton pushed out his lips and raised his head to the ceiling, trying to maintain his composure. *Well, this is awkward*, he thought. *And you used to be such a good liar, Stockton.*

He turned to the young man, a look of exaggerated surprise on his face. "Really, is that all? Well, that salary is downright insulting. That nice recruiter lady promised me at least $45,000."

The bald 30-something gave him a confused look before being called away by a woman from reception. He rose from his seat and walked briskly towards her, leaving Stockton alone.

I'm really losing my edge.

Directly opposite Stockton were two young Indian men seated beside each other. One was busily tapping away on a laptop while the other spoke in hushed tones on his phone. Given that they were speaking Indian, Stockton couldn't understand what they were saying, except for several mentions of Degner's name.

"Excuse me," he asked. "Do either of you gentlemen know Oran Degner?"

The man on the phone looked at him for a second but continued his call.

The laptop man replied. "Yes, we're meeting him today."

Stockton raised an eyebrow. "Really? You're meeting him here, at these offices?"

The laptop man kept his focus on the screen, typing frantically. "Yes, we're presenting a proposal to Mr. Degner this afternoon, why?"

A satisfied smile crossed Stockton's lips. He stood up and left the lobby with a spring in his step. He now had confirmation that Degner was physically in the building at that moment. All he had to do now was wait until the billionaire left the office that evening and doorstep him in the parking lot.

CHAPTER THREE

AFTER GRABBING a take-out lunch from the 1950s-themed diner across the street, Stockton returned to the sauna-like conditions of his car and slipped into the blistering heat of his leather-bound driver's seat. He cranked the AC to the max until the temperature came down. From here, he had an ideal vantage point from which to observe the front entrance of the Talaxacorp building.

He had no idea when Degner would finish work that evening, but he had a hunch that multi-billionaire CEOs probably had the luxury of not having to work as late as their underlings. He decided to take the opportunity to catch up on some news headlines on his phone and conduct some research on Degner.

As he swiped through the top stories of the day, his thumb landed upon an article about the global AI network. It discussed how politicians and expert scientists the world over were championing its reactivation as the panacea to all of humanity's current-day problems. The system would be coming online within days. It would have the ability to surveil all citizens and control their financial transactions for their alleged "safety and security" and to "ensure the most efficient usage of economic and environmental resources."

"Total slavery sold to us as utopia," He whispered under his breath. His stomach began to turn sour, and he was certain it wasn't the questionable chicken from his Caesar salad.

He opened a new browser window and began researching Degner. According to the man's Wiki profile, he'd been the CEO of Talaxacorp for nine years and was cited as the primary reason for the corporation's recent financial success. A former Wall Street hedge fund manager, communications tycoon, and real estate mogul, Degner was quite the corporate mover and shaker. Although he was respected by many in the business world, he also had his fair share of critics. His most vocal detractors labeled him a conman and a fraudster because of his checkered past in the world of multi-level marketing and what was essentially 'get rich quick' pyramid schemes.

Though he had been charged with fraud numerous times and came close to a considerable prison sentence, Degner's lawyers always seemed to get him off on some minor legal detail.

From the photographs he could find online, Stockton noticed a kind of soullessness in Degner's eyes. There was something about the man's physiognomy that just seemed a little off. His overly manicured grey hair and beard and extensive plastic surgery gave him an unnatural and almost inhuman visage. The man's smile harbored a disingenuous quality to it, like a sleazy, insincere smirk laced with duper's delight. Stockton wagered that given Degner's checkered past as a well-known hustler, it was entirely plausible that Talaxacorp was engaged in fraud of some kind.

But was the man capable of murder?

It seemed like a bit of a stretch. Nevertheless, he needed to come up with a ploy to encourage Degner to speak with him. He switched off his phone and returned to staring out the window at the Talaxacorp entrance.

And then it came to him. A smile grew across his face as he formulated his simple plan. But would it work?

BY 2:15 P.M., foot traffic in and out of the building had peaked after the late lunchers returned to the office. He sat patiently for another forty minutes or so and was gratified to find that his hunch had paid off.

Just before 3 p.m., a well-dressed middle-aged man wearing a grey Italian fashion suit and a pair of mirror sunglasses emerged from the revolving doors. He was accompanied by a young woman in a well-tailored red pants suit and a large, bald goliath of a man in a dark business casual outfit.

There was no mistaking that the man in the Italian suit was Degner. Stockton presumed the woman was his assistant and the linebacker-sized gentleman was his bodyguard. The three of them headed towards a black, tank-like SUV about 100 yards from the front entrance. As he sprung out of his vehicle, Stockton had to hoof it quickly across the parking lot to reach them before they got away.

"Mr. Degner!" Stockton hollered.

This immediately drew a suspicious and defensive glare from the bodyguard. Degner ignored Stockton at first, but after repeated calls, he glanced back and evaluated him.

"Mr. Degner, I'm not with the press, sir. I'm a private investigator. My name is Cody Stockton."

The stoney-faced bodyguard drew closer to Stockton while the personal assistant lady, carrying a personal organizer, motioned for Degner to ignore him and enter the vehicle by the rear passenger door.

"Sir, I'm investigating the death of one of your employees who worked in this building." Stockton held up the palms of his hands in a gesture that suggested he was of no threat.

The bodyguard briefly opened one side of his suit jacket to reveal a gun holstered on his hip. Stockton's heart rate increased dramatically, and his mouth became dry.

"I just want a moment of your time, sir. Can you speak to me about Eric Dallmeyer?" Stockton shouted while trying to maintain a friendly and harmless tone.

"Back it up!" The bodyguard aggressively replied as he stepped within ten feet of Stockton.

Stockton ignored the muscle man and maintained eye contact with Degner. He knew this doorstepping strategy was a high-risk gamble, but he remained confident his next move stood a good chance of being an ace in the hole.

"That's enough! Back it up!" The bodyguard pressed a firm hand the size of a bunch of bananas on Stockton's chest, pushing him back with considerable force.

"Please don't touch me," he replied defensively.

The Gorilla's patience was wearing thin.

"That's enough, sir. I have to ask you to leave the area."

Defiantly, Stockton raised his voice and played what he hoped would be a winning hand.

"Mr. Degner! I'd like to speak with you about Eric's death and his *findings*."

It was a solid bluff. If, in the unlikely event, Degner *did* have Eric murdered, then making Degner believe that Stockton was now in possession of Eric's evidence would be a powerful way of getting him to agree to an interview. Even if Eric's death had been a genuine accident, the danger that he had somehow smuggled evidence of fraud out of the building was probably too big a risk for Degner to ignore. This is why Stockton had placed considerable emphasis on the word "findings." It no doubt sounded just vague enough to be potentially ominous.

Degner stopped short of entering the SUV and turned to face Stockton. He buttoned his suit jacket and walked towards him, removing his shades.

"What's your name again?" Degner's voice was slightly raspy and nasally. Stockton wasn't certain, but he thought he detected a flicker of worry grow across the billionaire's waxy and synthetic face.

"Stockton, Cody Stockton. I'm investigating Eric's death. I'm looking to tie up some loose ends."

Degner tapped his designer sunglasses against the palm of his left hand and took about ten seconds before he replied.

"I never met Eric, but I hear he was a solid guy.

Great worker. Highly principled sorta person. Real shame what happened to the kid. Everyone's still hurtin' over his death, you know?"

Stockton found this reply most unusual. He thought back to what Olivia had told him earlier about how the CEO of Talaxacorp had told Eric to keep quiet about the scandal. Yet here was Degner claiming to have never met Eric. Stockton nodded and allowed a long, uncomfortable silence to pass in the hopes that Degner would feel the need to fill it.

"Look, ah, Mr. Stockton… I tell you what, I'm about to get on a plane right now. I'm back here on…" He turned to his assistant, now standing on his right side. "Suzie, when do we get back?"

"Friday morning," she replied swiftly.

"Okay, I'll tell you what." Degner's voice sounded almost solemn in its tone. "I'm back on Friday. You come out here and meet me at reception." He pointed at the front entrance with his shades. "Three o'clock, okay? I'll speak to you this Friday."

"That sounds great, Mr. Degner, thank you." Stockton noticed that the bodyguard never once took his eyes off him.

Degner nodded, and he and his two associates turned and headed back to the SUV.

That had gone better than Stockton could have hoped for. Friday was only two days away. In the meantime, he could search Eric Dallmeyer's home for any clues that might help the investigation. Maybe he might find something the police had missed.

OLIVIA HAD TEXTED Stockton the address for Eric's house, a 30-minute drive east of the industrial estate in a tranquil middle-class suburb. It was a little after 6 p.m. by the time he pulled up in the driveway of a modest but cozy two-bedroom bungalow. She'd swung by the house in the early evening before Stockton arrived and left him a key to the front door under the welcome mat.

As he let himself in the house and stepped into the wide, carpeted hallway, he was immediately greeted by an unpleasant, musty smell of stale, warm air. The air conditioning clearly hadn't been operational in a while. A framed mirror hung on the right-side wall just above a small table with an ornamental glass vase.

He flicked the nearest light switch in the hallway, but there was no response from the bulb in the ceiling. He entered the living room to the right of the hall and tried the light switch there. Once again, he was greeted with no illumination. Evidently, the electricity bill hadn't been paid in a while. Thankfully, there was still sufficient daylight streaming through the windows at this time of the evening.

He began his search for clues in the cozily decorated living room. The walls were adorned with salmon-colored wallpaper with a raised floral texture patterning. A large grey sectional sofa took up the right-hand side of the room and offered a comfortable seating area to enjoy the 70-inch television mounted to the opposite wall.

A quick search of the narrow bookshelf to the right of the television revealed a broad assortment of book genres, from literary classics, science fiction, thrillers, skydiving, self-help, occult, and spiritual/religious. Four volumes, in particular, stood out: *The Perils of Satanic Worship*, *Singularitas: The Nightmare Doctrine*, *Christian Homecoming: Returning to Jesus,* and *Satan: The Red Orb of Evil.* To Stockton, these books certainly made for a wacky collection of woo-woo.

Not exactly light reading, he thought, raising an eyebrow.

The only other notable book on the shelf was Oran Degner's autobiography. The cover had a suitably smug photo of the man standing in front of an expensive sports car and holding stacks of cash in his hands.

Stockton rolled his eyes. *The man has no shame.*

There was a large framed photograph of Eric on the left side wall. He was wearing his graduation gown, with a mortarboard on his head, a degree scroll in his hand, and a wide, toothy smile on his face. His parents stood on either side of him, beaming with obvious pride.

Stockton moved on and began searching the kitchen next. He found typical stuff: cupboards and drawers full of pots, pans, plates, cups, saucers, and kitchen utensils. The fridge, which was obviously no longer cool, contained a single jar of Thai curry paste, two bottles of non-alcoholic beer, and a slice of lemon, which was now heavily colonized by a blue, furry coating of mold. After determining the kitchen had nothing more to offer, he left the room and shut the door behind him.

Briefly poking his head into the well-appointed and spotlessly clean bathroom turned up nothing, as did the storage closet next to it. Beside the closet was a door to a narrow spare room that contained two single beds with an empty locker in between them.

The final door down the hall led to Eric's bedroom. The double bed was on the left-hand side. To the right was a row of wardrobes with mirrored sliding doors. Sliding open the first door panel revealed a pretty normal selection of men's clothes hanging from the rack.

Directly ahead of Stockton and to the left of the wardrobes was a desk with a computer monitor and printer, but there was no computer on the desk. He wondered where it was. Eric might have made use of a laptop, which could be somewhere at Talaxacorp.

He proceeded to rifle through the two drawers of the desk. The top drawer was home to a magazine about skydiving, three ballpoint pens, an elastic band, a USB charging cable, a small instruction manual for a Bluetooth speaker, and half a packet of cough lozenges.

In the second drawer, Stockton found a used cinema ticket, a brochure for a hotel in Cleveland, and a small crucifix. To the left of the desk was a chest of drawers filled with underwear, T-shirts, socks, and other sundries.

So far, diddly squat.

To the right of the desk was a larger bookshelf than the one in the living room. Again, nothing noteworthy stood out to him. He puffed his cheeks and let out a long, deep sigh. *Am I grasping at straws here?*

Slightly despondent, he glanced around the room for a moment. Looking back at the bookshelf, one of the volumes caught his eye. Along the spine of one particular book, read the title: *The Lord Will Guide You Forever*. It reminded Stockton of a Bible quote from the book of Isaiah.

He removed the book from the shelf and thumbed through it, shutting it suddenly to look back at the front cover. The name of the author on the book's cover read: *Eric Dallmeyer*. He flipped to the back cover, where there was a description and a small biography about the author:

Eric Dallmeyer is a devoted Christian and IT specialist based in Nevada. He is a passionate skydiver and has competed in base jumping competitions throughout North America. He converted to Christianity at the age of 23 and is a regular volunteer at his local Church.

This certainly threw Stockton for a loop. It turned out Eric was an author of Christian philosophy in his spare time. The young man was full of surprises.

As Stockton leafed through the book, a full-size sheet of paper fell out from the center pages and glided to the floor. He put the book on the desk for a moment and bent down to retrieve the page. It was a printed email. He studied it carefully:

Eric,

I want to thank you for bringing this to my attention. I'm absolutely livid with them for what they've done. I know I had my own selfish interests in all of this, but I had no idea what they were really doing behind the scenes. Please don't take the matter any further; these people are clearly highly dangerous and well-resourced. We don't truly know what we're dealing with. Let's keep this between the two of us for now, ok, buddy?

I've enlisted the services of a private investigator to look into what they've done. I'm going to meet with him tomorrow at my suite at the Baroque Haven Hotel and Casino.

I'll be in touch with you in a few days after I speak with him.

Best,

Oran

"WHAT THE HELL?" Stockton asked himself out loud.

He stood in silence, rereading the email several times. The date on the top of the page was February 27th, 2045, two days before Eric's fatal car crash. Stockton's mind began to spin. He sat down on the bed to gather his thoughts.

It turned out Degner had indeed been lying when he said he'd never met Eric, which was highly suspicious. Clearly, the two men knew each other. This aligned with what Olivia had told him earlier. From this email, it appeared that Eric had brought something to the attention of Degner, something that some person or persons had done, and Degner had hired a PI to find out more.

The email left Stockton with more questions than answers. He wondered what Degner had meant when he said, "I know I had my own selfish interests in all of this." He considered if that might be some kind of confession.

Stockton was curious as to who Degner was referring to when he wrote, "These people." He described them as "clearly dangerous and well-resourced." In Stockton's mind, these descriptions and the timing of Eric's death put murder firmly back on the table as a possibility. Was it possible that this unknown third party had murdered Eric? Was Degner in on it?

He folded the email and placed it inside his jacket pocket.

A compelling lead, at last.

It was now dark outside, requiring him to use his flashlight to navigate down the hallway. He planned on heading back to his apartment and calling it a day. Until he met with Degner again on Friday, all he could do in the meantime was wait.

As Stockton turned the corner in the main hallway and prepared to leave the bungalow, he noticed that the door to the kitchen was slightly ajar.

He was certain he had closed it after he'd left the room earlier. He found he was now second-guessing himself. None of the windows were open, so there was no source of draft that could have caused the door to close over.

He cautiously pushed the door open fully and stepped back inside the kitchen. It was just as he'd left it. He turned back into the hallway and concluded he was being paranoid. He briefly considered the possibility that Olivia had returned, but he would have heard her reenter the house. Besides, he could see through the foyer windows on either side of the front door. His car was still the only one parked in the driveway.

He crossed the hallway and reached for the handle of the front door. For a microsecond, he thought he briefly saw a reflection of something moving in the glass of the foyer window. At precisely that moment, he heard what sounded like a footstep from behind him.

I'm not alone!

Before he had another split second to react, Stockton was violently grabbed hard by the neck from behind and flung against the left side wall of the hallway with considerable force. His forehead smacked against the wall. He crumpled to the floor in agony. He was dazed and in a frantic blur of confusion and terror. Large leather-clad hands wrapped themselves tightly around his neck and began squeezing his windpipe.

He instinctively grabbed at the hands. The attacker now lay on top of him with a knee buried agonizingly in his back. With a considerable exertion of every ounce of his physical strength, Stockton pushed himself up a few inches off the floor using his hands and knees. He jerked his neck quickly to deliver a swift back headbutt on his attacker. The blow struck the person directly on the nose. They stumbled backward.

Adrenaline coursed through his veins as he staggered to his feet and began to reach for his gun in his concealed carry shoulder holster. He turned to face his opponent, a tall, broad man dressed entirely in black, wearing a balaclava. He spotted Stockton's gun under his jacket and rose quickly, lunging at him with his left fist. The detective effectively dodged the blow by quickly stepping off to the man's outside. He then countered with a powerful left jab of his own. He planted the punch squarely into the man's stomach. The impact forced the attacker to stumble momentarily and fall flat onto his back with a groan of pain.

Stockton, now standing over him, attempted to capitalize. He brought his right fist down hard on the man's face. The attacker blocked the punch with the elbow of his left arm.

Stockton attempted to take a second swing at him. The man reacted with lightning speed and precision. He quickly placed his left foot under Stockton's right knee, gripping tightly. With his right leg pressed against his hip, he pushed Stockton off balance and rolled him on the floor with a heavy thud.

The man scrambled to get back to his feet. Stockton began kicking wildly on the floor, trying unsuccessfully to sweep the man with his left leg. His opponent responded by firmly planting his right foot into Stockton's stomach. This caused him to flip over onto his back, forcing the wind out of his chest.

The man then reached down and grabbed Stockton by his shirt collar and proceeded to lift him off the floor. He reared his neck back and prepared to finish the detective with a final head butt. Stockton grabbed the glass vase off the hallway table with his left hand. He smashed it directly into the man's face.

The attacker wailed in agony. He released his grip on Stockton's collar and dropped him to the floor. He placed his hands on his aching, mask-covered face, which now had small fragments of glass embedded in it.

Stockton slowly began to rise to his feet again and reached under his jacket for his gun. The man swung around and grabbed the front door handle. He flung it open and dashed down the driveway and out into the street.

Holding his chest in pain, Stockton tore after him with his gun in hand. Reaching the sidewalk, he raised the weapon and attempted to aim at his fleeing attacker, but the blow to his head had destabilized his equilibrium, making a clear shot impossible.

A screech of car brakes echoed around the housing estate. A black, mid-sized van came careening around the corner and stopped halfway down the street. The side door slipped open, and the large black-clad man, still nursing his injured face with his right hand, clumsily jumped inside, sliding the door closed behind him. The van sped off down the street. Stockton holstered his weapon and managed to capture a photo of the van's license plate with his phone camera just before it disappeared out of sight.

Shaken, battered, and bruised, and still trying to catch his breath, Stockton sat down on the grass outside the driveway of Eric Dallmeyer's home. His mind was racing and trying to process what he'd just been through. Whoever had jumped him must have been somehow connected to Eric's death. He noticed several of the neighbors had now come onto the street to see what the commotion was all about.

The aches and pains in his body only increased as the adrenaline began to subside and his breathing and heart rate gently reduced. He unlocked his smartphone again and dialed Ridgemore directly on his personal number. After the fourth ring, the old cop picked up.

"Cody, I swear this had better be good if you're calling me at home while I'm watching an episode of McQuaid with my family."

"Sorry, Devon," Stockton wheezed. "The situation is far from good."

A concerned tone entered Ridgemore's voice. "What's the matter with you? You sound like you've been running up a flight of stairs…"

Stockton winced again at the pains in his head and his side. "I think you'll have to reopen your file on Eric Dallmeyer after all."

"What makes you say that?"

"Because," Stockton replied, looking at the photo of the black van on his smartphone. "I'm fairly certain he was murdered."

CHAPTER
FOUR

RIDGEMORE LEANED CLOSELY against the wall in the hallway where Stockton's face had been smacked against. He rapped it lightly with his fist. From the sound it made, he could tell the wall was a hollow partition. He then tried the wall on the opposite side, which felt like solid concrete all the way through.

"You're lucky he didn't smash your head against *this* wall, or we wouldn't be here talkin' right now." Ridgemore appraised the hallway while forensics people began busily examining every surface in the house for the intruder's fingerprints and hair follicles.

It was just after 8:15 p.m., and three police cruisers and an ambulance were now parked outside of Eric Dallmeyer's driveway. The street was abuzz with crowds of neighbors gathered at the scene, and a few witnesses were giving statements to police officers. The darkened hallway of the house was lit only by the intermittent flashing blue light from the police cars outside.

"Sorry for taking you away from the exciting crime-fighting adventures of Detective Keith McQuaid." Stockton half-muttered sarcastically as a paramedic shone a bright light into his eyes.

"Ah, don't worry about it, Carolyn said we'd already watched that episode anyways. I didn't remember it at all, but she never forgets anything," he confessed as he stood in the hallway sipping his coffee and watching his men work.

"Especially all the anniversaries you've forgotten," Stockton quipped.

Ridgemore grumbled, "That only happened once."

The broad-shouldered detective cut quite an imposing presence in the hallway. A formidable and stocky bear of a man at six feet four, Ridgemore was a good two inches taller than Stockton. White and grey hairs peppered his temples and goatee, a weathered quality to his skin, and harshness to his deep-set brown eyes complemented his no-nonsense personality. His long, dark blue trench coat had become an almost iconic part of his identity, which he wore regardless of the weather. Stockton affectionately likened it to being a kind of superhero outfit, like a suit of armor that transformed Ridgemore into the seasoned, tough-as-nails detective that criminals feared.

"Thanks for coming over so quickly all the same." Stockton was seated in the hall on one of the chairs from the kitchen with a bag of ice applied to his swollen right hand.

The young male paramedic wiped down Stockton's inflamed forehead with a warm cloth. "Nothing appears to be broken," he said. "But there are some signs of a minor concussion. I'd like to keep you in overnight just as a precaution."

"I'll be fine, thank you," Stockton replied softly. "I reckon I'll just head home and get some sleep."

"For God's sake, Cody! Can you ever just do what you're told?" Ridgemore squawked. "Go to the hospital and get that damn head of yours checked out properly! You could end up croakin' in your sleep with brain swelling, for Heaven's sake!"

"I appreciate the concern, Devon, but I've had worse. I'm just grateful that the vase was within arm's reach, or I'd probably be dead by now." Stockton pointed with his chin toward the fragments of glass strewn throughout the carpet.

"Fine!" Ridgemore's nostrils flared. "But I swear, if you wake up dead tomorrow, I'll kill you myself!"

Stockton looked at Ridgemore incredulously.

"Yeah, because everything about that sentence made sense."

Ridgemore took a sip of his coffee. "The guy you tussled with, do you think he wanted to kill you?"

"I believe so. I can handle myself in a fight, but he had mixed martial arts training for sure. He was definitely sent to end me."

Ridgemore's face scrunched into an expression that suggested skepticism. "I doubt it. For all we know, he was just a burglar, and you were in the wrong place at the wrong time."

"A burglar?" Stockton's voice rose a few octaves. "Really? If the guy *was* an opportunistic burglar, he would have run out the door as soon as he saw me. But instead, this guy actively tried to choke me to death and displayed a level of combat training I haven't seen since the war."

"Uh oh, watch out! We're gonna get a war story next from the veteran!" Ridgemore teased as he shot a glance at the paramedic.

"It was no damn burglar Devon! Degner must have had the guy follow me here with instructions to murder me when he had the chance. Degner's the only person at Talaxacorp who knew I was investigating Eric's case."

Ridgemore was taken aback. "You spoke to Oran Degner?"

"Yes, earlier this afternoon. I asked him about

Eric, and he claimed he didn't know him, which was a lie." Stockton reached into his inside jacket pocket.

"How do you know that?"

"Because of this." Stockton handed Ridgemore the sheet of paper he found inside Eric's book. "It's correspondence between Degner and Eric about some dangerous people they'd unwittingly gotten involved with. Degner said he was hiring a PI to investigate them. Take a look at the date at the top of the email header."

Ridgemore quietly read the email with the aid of a flashlight due to the low light of the hallway. He mouthed the words under his breath as his eyes ran across the page.

"Sounds like Degner got involved in somethin' suspect, and Eric was possibly going to spill the beans about it. If Eric *was* murdered, the question is, was it Degner who did it or these 'highly dangerous, well-resourced' people he mentions here?"

"My guess would be Degner." Stockton ventured. "The fact that he lied about not knowing Eric is a red flag, in my opinion. I'm due to speak with Degner when he returns from some business trip on Friday."

"Hmm. I won't lie, this does change the complexion of things a bit. I thought I told you not to give me any more damn paperwork, Cody?" He placed the page into the front pocket of his trench coat.

"Sorry, Devon, but it appears that Eric's death is going to need another look. Oh, and you might want to take a gander at this license plate."

Stockton unlocked his phone and tapped a couple of times to call up the photo he'd taken of the rear of the getaway van.

Ridgemore took the phone in his hands and squinted at the image. "Can you email that image to *my* phone?"

"Already done," Stockton said as he stood up and prepared to leave.

Ridgemore handed him back his device.

"Okay, we'll run that plate and see what comes up. Meantime, go home and get some rest. We'll discuss our next move tomorrow morning and don't even think about driving your car home. If I see you so much as sit in that driver's seat, I'll book you faster than my first wife can spend my alimony payments on shoes and lip filler injections."

Ridgemore pointed to a uniformed cop standing just outside the doorway. "Norman, drive Cody home in his car, will ya? And have Pérez follow behind you in a cruiser."

"I appreciate it, Devon, thanks." Stockton yawned as he walked past Ridgemore towards the front door.

"Cody, it Looks like you may have stumbled into somethin' a bit more than you bargained for."

Stockton looked back at the older man from the

doorway and briefly glanced at the broken glass on the floor. His mind flashed back to the traumatic, violent ordeal he'd endured only minutes earlier.

"Yeah, it sure as heck looks that way."

Stockton turned and stepped out into the balmy Nevada night.

LESS THAN AN HOUR LATER, Stockton was staring out the passenger side window of his car as Officer Richard Norman drove them down the strip at a leisurely pace. All along the south end, the protest groups had largely dispersed by that stage of the evening. They were reduced to just a few small and increasingly weary pockets of noisemakers holding signs and chanting with noticeably less enthusiasm along portions of the I-15.

Over the low volume of the car radio, he could just about make out one of the chants. "Say it loud, say it clear, we don't want your AI here!"

Some of the protester's placards contained such messages as: "No AI in Nevada!", "Shut Down the Machine!" and "Keep America Free! Abolish Artificial Intelligence!"

He hoped and prayed they could be successful in their activism against the incoming control grid, but as each day passed, it felt like they were fighting a losing battle.

The streets were buzzing with the energy of party-goers, people watchers, gamblers, ramblers, and all sorts. Stockton usually enjoyed taking in the bright lights emanating from the jaw-dropping mega resorts and themed hotels of Sin City, but not tonight. His mind was adrift in an ocean of disparate thoughts concerning his case.

Had Degner really attempted to have me killed?

Who were the mysterious people he referred to in his email to Eric? What was the scandal being covered up at Talaxacorp?

Every so often, he was shifted out of his ruminations by the aches and pains in his body, especially his bandaged right hand. He attempted once again to close it into a half-fist, but the swelling and wince-inducing agony in his stiff knuckles made that impossible.

As they drove past the opulent high-rise towers of the City Center area, he caught sight of a few protesters finishing up for the evening and placing their placards and signs into the back of a van.

Stockton's attention was broken by the intrusion of a female news anchor on the radio with a bulletin.

"The President has recently returned from a meeting of International leaders in Geneva, where a finalized agreement has been reached to accelerate the activation of the dormant AI system. The revised date has now moved forward to Friday of next week."

Stockton and Norman looked at each other in disbelief.

The report continued. "The AI will be given significant control over regulating environmental, industrial, and economic resources in order to efficiently manage human civilization."

Stockton was stunned. It wasn't difficult to understand the substantial public backlash to the plan. The same AI that had enslaved humanity and genocided a billion people would soon have all the power it needed to do it again. At the bare minimum, it would likely become an authoritarian menace in people's lives.

Why the hell did we fight a war against AI if the bloody thing is about to take over the world anyway?

"I got an aunt in Florida," Norman broke into Stockton's thoughts. "She says the protests in downtown Tallahassee have turned super violent. Burned-out police vehicles, smashed-up buildings, and local politicians were assaulted. It's getting wild in some parts of the country. After *this* news, I can't imagine how much worse it's gonna get."

"Governments refusing to listen to their people, the oldest story in politics," Stockton proffered mournfully as Las Vegas Boulevard flashed past his distracted eyes in a blur of neon and LED lights.

The radio once again jolted him from his quiet contemplation. "An extraordinary story from Argentina next. Locals in one small town North of Mendoza have described how a mysterious man claiming to be Jesus Christ, the Son of God, has been performing miracles and healing the sick. The man who…"

Norman slapped the on/off switch of the car radio, and the voice disappeared. "What a crock of nonsense! Probably another conman cult leader scamming poor naive fools out of their money or somethin'…"

"Yeah, the world certainly has no shortage of willing suckers," Stockton snorted.

Fifteen minutes later, they arrived outside of Stockton's apartment complex south of Freemont. Norman parked the car across the street and took a lift back to the station with Pérez, who'd been following them in a police vehicle.

Exhausted and struggling through a pounding headache and numerous bodily contusions, Stockton had firmly set his mind on a double whiskey and face-planting into his bed for a long, comatose slumber.

After taking the elevator to his third-floor apartment, he slipped the key in the front door and unlocked it. He instinctively reached for the light switch on the left-side wall, only to find that the lights were already on.

"Oh, Thank God," came Zara's voice from the kitchen. Her loud footsteps thundered through the apartment as she briskly rounded the corner and entered the hallway to greet him.

The sheer sight of her was enough to rejuvenate him somewhat and make him feel almost normal.

He immediately noticed a perturbed look on her face as she caught sight of his facial bruises and swelling. She gently placed her cool, soft hand on his cheek and then over his slightly inflamed forehead.

"Good Lord, Baby, is it very painful?"

"It's okay. Nothing, a few painkillers, and some shuteye won't fix." He began to remove his jacket.

"Here, let me help you."

She moved behind him and gingerly slid his swollen, wrapped hand through the cuff of his jacket's right sleeve, being careful not to disturb the bandages. "Come in and sit down. I'll make you some tea."

She swiftly darted to the kitchen, leaving Stockton to slump onto the living room couch. He could hear her running the tap and filling the kettle with water.

"I brought turmeric. It's great for inflammation." She hollered.

Stockton slouched onto the sofa and closed his

eyes. He was exhausted. "And some painkillers, please. By the way, how did you know about what happened?"

She returned to the living room, drying her hands with a towel.

"Ridgemore called me. He said some guy jumped you. I got a cab straight over here. I've been worried sick. What the hell happened?"

"Turns out the case I'm working on isn't quite as simple, neat, and tidy as I'd naively presumed." Stockton couldn't help but chuckle, though his ribs ached slightly when he did.

"And what about all that talk before about being more careful out there? About not taking on such dangerous work?" Zara unconsciously stroked the crucifix at the end of her necklace with her forefinger and thumb. She stared at him with a deeply distressed expression on her face.

Stockton didn't have the energy to conceive of an adequately comforting response. He simply shrugged and stared down at his injured right hand.

Zara released a frustrated exhale and returned to the kitchen.

After a few moments, she called back to him in a voice loud enough so he could still hear her. "Can you at least tell me the cops are gonna catch this guy, right?"

"They're workin' on it, sweetheart." Stockton had

to force the words out, as he was so utterly spent. "Look, it's going to be okay. I'll be much more careful next time."

She returned to the living room carrying an ice pack, a mug full of peppermint tea, and two painkiller tablets and handed them to him. She took a seat on the sofa cushion to his left.

"You'll press charges and sue the hell out of this guy when they do catch him?"

Stockton swallowed the two tablets with a sip of his tea. "Hmm."

"You don't seem too confident that the police will be able to find him?" She gently stroked the back of his head with her right hand.

He took another sip and looked at her earnestly. "These people are professionals, Zara, and they don't often make mistakes."

"What the hell have you gotten involved with?"

He stared at the tea bag floating in his mug and then fixed his gaze directly into her eyes. "I have a feeling I'm going to find out soon enough."

IT SOUNDED for all the world like a siren was going off. Stockton was disoriented and confused as he awoke in the darkness with no idea where he was. He frantically jumped out of bed and stumbled around the room before he realized his phone was ringing.

"What's going on?" asked Zara groggily from her side of the bed.

Reaching for his device in the dark, Stockton stubbed his toe against the dressing table and let out a series of colorful expletives. He could see from the phone that the time was 6:32 a.m. He'd been asleep for just under seven hours. He tapped the screen and answered the call. It was from Ridgemore.

"Devon, what is it? What's wrong?" Stockton could feel his heart pumping hard through his chest.

"Cody, you awake?" came Ridgemore's voice over the phone.

"No, of course not," he snapped irritably. "I'm still fast asleep, and I just happen to have the ability to answer the phone when I'm unconscious."

"Ok, ok, don't get your boxers in a bunch. We got a situation."

"What is it? What's happened?"

"You seen the news?"

"Devon, I've literally just told you that you've woken me up. How could I possibly have seen the news already? Can you please tell me why you're calling so early?" Stockton thundered exasperatedly.

"Right, right. Look, um, they found Oran Degner," Ridgemore replied somberly.

"And? Has anyone questioned him?"

"He won't be answering any more questions, I'm afraid. The guy's dead. Police found his body in his hotel room in Toronto."

Stockton blinked hard and rubbed his temples. His mouth opened, but no words came out. His still-sleeping synapses were struggling to process the information.

Ridgemore sighed. "He was murdered."

CHAPTER FIVE

"MURDERED? WHAT?" Stockton's mind was still spinning, and he was fairly certain it wasn't his head injury.

Zara switched on her bedside light, and Stockton's eyes struggled momentarily to adjust to the sudden blinding change in illumination.

"Babe, what's happening? Who's been murdered?" she asked fearfully, sitting up in the bed.

"Give me a moment, Zara," Stockton replied, leaving the bedroom and walking into his office across the hall.

"Devon, what happened?" He tapped the loudspeaker button on the phone and began nervously pacing the room.

Ridgemore took a gulp of some beverage and continued. "The cops said Degner was found drowned in the bathtub of his hotel room. They think the intention was to make it look like suicide because of the mess load of sleeping pills the murderer had accidentally dropped when he fled the scene. He had entered the room through the balcony while Degner was bathing, but he panicked when Degner's valet walked in on him through the front door."

"And then what happened?" Stockton's mind was rapidly trying to visualize the scene.

"The valet saw the guy, ran back down the hall to get help, and that's when the murderer switched to plan B. He burst into the bathroom and probably caught Degner off guard. Plunged his head under the water and drowned him. By the time security arrived at the room, the intruder was gone, and all that was left was a bunch of sleeping pills on the carpet and a dead billionaire in the hot tub. The story's all over the news, nauseating tributes pouring in from celebs and politicians all morning."

Stockton took a seat at his desk and tried to marshall his thoughts. "Did the valet identify the guy?"

"Nope, his face was covered."

Stockton drummed his fingers on the desk.

"I was supposed to meet him tomorrow at Talaxacorp."

"Looks like someone didn't want that meeting to take place. I think we can conclude that whoever these folks were who killed Eric also killed Degner and tried to kill you too. You might want to start wearin' a vest under your shirt, just in case."

"More importantly, I'm now worried about both Zara and my client. For all we know, someone's been watching Olivia Dallmeyer for some time. They may have followed me from her house. Her life could be in danger. And they could try to get to me through Zara."

"I'll put a few uniforms on watch at Olivia's place, your place, and your girlfriend's. Best I can do." Ridgemore tried to sound as reassuring as possible.

"Thanks, Devon, that's appreciated." Stockton leaned back in his chair, stared at the ceiling fan, and began to think out loud. "So Degner wasn't behind Eric's murder, which means he obviously didn't send someone to kill me. He must have been working closely with Eric to investigate whatever scandal had taken place at the company. When Eric was murdered, Degner must have gotten scared off."

"That would explain why he denied knowing Eric when he spoke to you yesterday," Ridgemore added.

"If that's the case, if Degner was trying to keep his head down and stay quiet about the scandal to save his own skin, then… " A pang of guilt struck Stockton in the heart.

"Then you reopened the can of worms when you started poking your head into Eric's murder. Degner might have thought he could confide something in you…" Ridgemore took another audible gulp of his drink.

Stockton let out a long exhale. "It's possible my involvement in the case is what got Degner killed. Whoever these people are, they were worried he was going to talk to me."

"You can't blame yourself, Cody, you didn't know what you didn't know. He isn't dead because of you. This whole situation just stinks to high Heaven. Smells worse than the green gunk underneath my ingrown toenail."

Stockton grimaced with disgust. "I could have done without that image, Devon."

He stood up from his desk and walked towards the window, gazing out across the Downtown area as the early sunrise began to brighten the dawn sky. "I guess this means the investigation into Eric's death is going to be reopened?"

"Like you even need to ask that question at this point? The information in the email you found and the timing of the deaths point to a broader conspiracy now. Two very suspicious deaths within six weeks of each other, connected by some kind of unknown wrongdoing at Talaxacorp. It's got double homicide written all over it. But all I can officially do is investigate *Eric's* death because Degner was killed outside of the country. I've got to pass on everything

I have to Interpol for the international portion of the investigation. I'm hoppin' on a conference call with one of their guys later this afternoon. Damn it, at some point, I've got to find a couple of minutes to sleep."

Stockton contemplatively ran his index finger across his mustache. "The answers we're looking for might very well be found inside the Talaxacorp offices or at Degner's home."

"We'll be searchin' both premises in short order. In the meantime, it's best you let your client know that the cops have officially taken over the investigation into Eric's death. But I could still use a leg man if you're interested in stayin' on the case. Plenty of avenues you could still pursue on your end."

"I really appreciate that, Devon. Actually, it just so happens I have one such avenue in mind."

STOCKTON EXPLAINED the situation to Zara over breakfast. He tried to assuage her concerns for their safety by telling her about the police protection assigned to watch her home. This provided her with some degree of peace of mind. She offered to help him cover up the visible cuts and bruises on his face with some concealer, but Stockton explained how he'd rather die of explosive decompression than wear women's makeup. He settled for a pair of shades and a baseball cap instead.

After dropping her off at work, he made his way to the hottest and most luxurious new 5-star resort on the strip, the Baroque Haven Hotel and Casino, where Oran Degner had been renting a suite.

It was 9:15 a.m., and already the temperature had reached a comfortable 67 degrees in what felt like the beginning of an early summer. April in Vegas brought with it the return of pool party season, which provided a substantial and noticeable bump in tourists across the city. Hordes of twenty and thirty-somethings flocked to the desert valley to soak up the sumptuous Nevada sunshine in their bathing suits. The partygoers would lounge on day beds, rent expensive cabanas, sip fancy cocktails, and listen to their favorite world-famous DJs by the Strip's most opulent swimming pools.

Oh, to be young again!

While the economy certainly benefited from the extra vacationers all looking for the quintessential Vegas experience, overcrowding in the city's most touristy hotspots became a frustrating but inevitable side effect.

The congestion was only worsened by the addition of a substantial number of protesters who'd staged an anti-AI demonstration at the front of the building. The underground parking garage at the

Baroque Haven was close to bursting point by the time Stockton spied an empty spot after thirty minutes of circling in his vehicle.

A basement escalator took him to a long walkway, which eventually led to a fifteen-second elevator ride to the floor above. The elevator doors parted to reveal a sweeping hotel foyer bedecked in stunning 11th-century Romanesque architectural stylings fused with late 19th-century English Victorian design. The effect was a dizzyingly ornate and ostentatious merger of two highly decorative classical eras.

Stockton felt as though he had suddenly been transported to St Peter's Basilica in Rome or St Paul's Cathedral in London. He was overwhelmed by the sheer scale, beauty, and attention to detail of the mesmerizing spectacle all around him. The foyer had become a popular tourist attraction that drew large crowds regardless of whether they were staying at the hotel or not.

I could never afford to stay a single night in this place.

Making his way through the masses of sightseers and selfie-takers, he reached the entrance to the casino at the far end of the foyer. The casino was brightly lit, which was a nice contrast to some of the older, dingier properties on the strip.

He moved briskly past the labyrinthian rows of slot machines being played by hundreds of zombified gamblers, mindlessly emptying their hard-earned cash into the coffers of corporate shareholders. As with any casino, it was a visual and auditory sea of flashing lights, large LED touchscreens, beeps, and jingly jangling noises. He then strode through the table games section next, which was much less popular at this time of the day.

On the periphery of the casino were hallways leading to the shopping mall area and the various bars, lounges, and fine dining restaurants of the hotel. These were the kinds of overpriced and pretentious venues that locals like Stockton avoided like the plague, except, of course, when Zara was in the mood to be spoiled with a fancy night out.

All told the hike from the parking garage to the suitably lavish front desk area took Stockton eighteen minutes.

Only in Vegas can you walk forever and get basically nowhere.

He spoke with an incredibly friendly and helpful Assistant Manager named Kyle and explained that he was investigating the murders of Eric Dallmeyer and Oran Degner. Kyle promptly confirmed Stockton's identity and police vetting with a quick phone call to Ridgemore's assistant. He was escorted to Degner's suite by a pleasant security guard named Chip. Degner's suite was on the 53rd floor of the main tower and was accessed by a dedicated high-speed elevator with an acceleration and deceleration force so great that Stockton's sensitive stomach just barely managed to contain his breakfast.

He was informed that Degner had rented the two-bedroom penthouse apartment for the past eight months at the eye-watering price of $22,000 per night. Stockton attempted a quick calculation in his mind but began to struggle with carrying all those zeros and concluded it was more money than he could earn in a lifetime.

Management had planned to remove Degner's personal effects and hold them for a family member to collect, but the police had frozen access to the suite as part of the investigation. Stockton had unlimited time to search for clues.

Chip unlocked the front door and waited outside as Stockton entered the 3,600 square foot, two-story penthouse.

Okay, Degner. What secrets have you left for me to find?

He found himself standing on the upper level of the two-story suite on a balcony that doubled as a living area. Looking down from the balcony, he saw a beautifully appointed primary living space below with lavish sofas, a pool table, and a large paladin window with a spectacular view of the Baroque Haven golf course and Mount Charleston in the distance.

Placing his hands on the railing of the balcony, he

mulled a few things over in his mind. Six weeks earlier, Degner had met with a PI in this very suite and hired him to investigate some mysterious third party. A group who'd murdered Eric Dallmeyer to prevent him from exposing their secret activities at Talaxacorp.

What scandal could possibly have justified the killing of Eric and a powerful billionaire?

To his right and left were hallways that led to the bedrooms. The hallway to his right also led to an ornate staircase to the lower level. He took that hallway first and entered a bedroom.

The room was decorated in a Victorian period style with Gothic and Elizabethan design elements in the furniture, wall paneling, and ceiling moldings. A king-sized four-poster bed dominated the room, complete with a deep button-upholstered headboard and a silk duvet. The hardwood floors were authentic mahogany that looked freshly varnished.

He opened every drawer, cabinet, and wardrobe in the room to find nothing but a hairdryer and a Bible.

This must be the guest bedroom. Probably not much to find here.

The gigantic bathroom looked more like a high-end spa, with marbled floors, a four-person jacuzzi tub, a steam shower, and a sauna.

He exited the guest bedroom, walked down the

hallway, and passed the balcony once again. This hallway led to a few other noteworthy rooms, including a 10-seater cinema and a small gym, which was home to a treadmill and cross trainer.

This isn't the kind of exercise Zara and I would get up to if we had a suite like this for a night.

The next door led to the other bedroom, which was identical to the first in every detail, with the exception that it had clearly been in use fairly recently.

This looks a bit more promising.

Stockton found both men's and women's clothes hanging in the wardrobes. He looked through the left bedside locker, which contained a photograph of a topless Degner in swimming shorts with his arm around a beautiful bikini-clad brunette lady. They were standing on a beach. There was also an empty jewelry box, hand moisturizer, a jar of strawberry-flavored lip balm, a room key card, a packet of sanitary towels, and an expensive pair of wireless headphones. This drawer obviously belonged to the lady.

He moved swiftly to the other side of the bed and began searching through Degner's locker. Inside, he found a USB wall socket adaptor, an empty hip flask, a receipt for a round of golf, a pair of smart glasses, a ballpoint pen with the Talaxacorp logo on it, and a stack of poker chips.

Moving from the bedroom into the walk-in

wardrobe, Stockton located the room safe, which was built directly into the wall. He tried the handle and confirmed it was sealed shut.

The safe was a Zalitrom 7400 series, which didn't make use of a conventional physical keypad. It could only be unlocked by entering the five-digit code using the Zalitrom app via a smartphone. The hotel guest would download the app and scan the QR code on the side of the safe, which would sync the safe to their device. Next, the guest would create their five-digit code.

For all he knew, the safe was empty anyway, but he was still eager to take a look inside. Unlocking a high-tech safe like this one was going to need some serious IT expertise.

He pulled out his smartphone, opened the address book, and located the name *Brock Haggard*. He sighed and winced at the same time and then tapped the phone icon to dial the number. It began to ring.

Brock Haggard was a particularly questionable associate of Stockton's from one of his previous cases. The man had a checkered past and a habit of sailing a little too close to the wind from a legal perspective. He was a retired professional hacktivist and former felon who had a background in military-grade IT counter-surveillance systems. He'd worked as a mercenary for hire for several private organizations to crack the security systems of rival companies.

Stockton hated the idea of calling the guy on the phone because he had a strong suspicion all of Haggard's calls were being monitored. He was also 90% certain the man was an actual certifiable psychopath, but he was also extremely well-connected, resourceful, and intelligent. He also just happened to owe Stockton a favor.

"Stockton! Long time no see, good to hear you're still alive, at least," came the low, gravelly voice of Haggard.

"Hello Brock. I could say the same." The tension in Stockton's voice was palpable.

"You back in the States then? Helluva job over there in London those years back, eh? How long ago was that? Like five or six?" Haggard's tone was cool as ice but with a low-grade menace about it.

"Seven, but who's counting?" Stockton said plainly.

"Seven years? Lordy, where does the time go? Say, we made a great team, didn't we? Me with the brains and you with the brawn. That was a fun little caper. It was pretty lucrative, as I seem to recall."

"Not exactly how I remember it, Brock."

Haggard guffawed so loudly down the phone Stockton had to pull the handset away from his ear. "Ah, Stockton, you're still the uptight, straight-laced gumshoe, aren't ya? You never did learn to lighten up. What can I do for ya anyways?"

Recomposing himself, Stockton explained.

"I'm at the Baroque Haven, and I've got a Zalitrom safe here that I'm trying to access. I know a lot of Vegas hotels make use of the same security contractors. I'm wondering if you might know…"

"Say no more, my tightly-wound little friend," Haggard cut in. "Gimme five minutes."

The phone went dead.

Stockton sighed, already regretting making the call.

He used the time to look around the room once again. The bathroom was much the same as the other one, except for a few personal items by the sink, such as toiletries and a woman's pink dressing gown hanging on the back of the door.

He reconsidered the wisdom of relying on a shady character like Haggard. The man had served twelve years in a minimum security prison and, to this day, has remained on several government watchlists and was banned from nineteen countries. The guy's hacking talents were so legendary that the prosecutor at his trial said he should be jailed for life because, in his words, "He could probably use a toaster to hack into your bank account."

After a couple of minutes of impatiently pacing around the bedroom, the phone rang.

"Yeah?" Stockton answered.

"Okay!" Haggard half-belched down the phone. "The guy I know who does the installations for Baroque, Castelmezzano, Diamond Canyon Hotel, and about six other joints on the strip says that there's a factory default code that can unlock the safe. Trouble is most of the hotels change the code themselves, so this mightn't work."

Stockton downloaded the Zalitrom app on his phone. He then grabbed a pen and hotel refill pad from the desk in the bedroom and wrote down the instructions Haggard gave him.

"First, scan the QR code using the app and sync 'em up."

Stockton did as he was instructed.

Haggard continued. "Next, you want to tap on the keypad button and triple-tap the pound key until four zeros flash on the display. Then enter the following sequence: Eight—eight—two—six—two—nine—zero—four—eight—seven—five. Then press pound again."

Stockton did what he was told, but nothing happened, the safe remained locked. "Damn, looks like they must have changed the code!"

"You sure you entered the numbers correctly?" Haggard asked calmly.

Stockton tried once again and hit the pound button. This time, the safe's locking mechanism disengaged, and the LED display flashed with red letters that read: "OPEN."

"It worked! Nice job, Brock! I'm in!"

"There you go, Stockton! What'd I tell ya? Brains and brawn once again," Haggard said jovially.

"Thank you, Brock."

"Oh, don't mention it. When I need a favor, I'll know who to call." Haggard's tone sounded almost ominous. The phone went dead.

Stockton hoped his brief reacquaintance with Haggard wouldn't come back and bite him in the ass at some point.

He turned the handle of the safe and looked inside. The contents were a literal treasure trove with some expensive-looking women's jewelry, several thousand dollars in cash, and a set of keys for a high-end sports car. Underneath these items sat a brown manilla envelope, which Stockton removed from the safe and opened to find a sheet of paper inside. It was a receipt. He looked it over carefully, and his heart started to flutter. He grinned widely.

Jackpot!

It was exactly what he'd been looking for.

He returned to the hallway, passed the balcony, and down the stairs to the living space. A cursory search of the drawers and cabinets there didn't reveal anything important. Likewise, the kitchenette, butler's pantry, and downstairs toilet offered nothing of value.

He returned to the living room and looked at the sheet of paper once again. It was a receipt for the services of a local private investigator by the name of Mickey Chambers. This was the man Degner had hired to investigate the scandal at Talaxacorp. Stockton was likely standing in the exact spot where Chambers and Degner had conducted their meeting just a few days before Eric was killed. He wondered how that conversation had gone.

Did Degner show any signs of being afraid for his own life?

With a little luck, this Chambers fellow might have some useful information that could lead to identifying the killers of both men.

CHAPTER SIX

AFTER LEAVING the Baroque Haven Hotel and Casino, Stockton opted to head home and make contact with Mickey Chambers to arrange a meeting. Chambers was wary of Stockton at first and didn't want to speak over the phone. After some convincing, he eventually agreed to meet the next day in a public place.

Stockton had little else to do, so he met Zara for lunch downtown and then spent much of the rest of the afternoon watching news reports about the death of Oran Degner.

Ridgemore phoned in the late evening to reveal that the license plate of the getaway van was from a vehicle reported stolen three weeks earlier. A dead end. Stockton informed him of his upcoming meeting with Chambers and agreed to keep him in the loop.

The next morning began with a light sprinkling of rain, which gave way to a warm and mostly overcast afternoon. Stockton ambled down the pedestrianized Freemont street, sheltered from the occasional shower thanks to the enormous LED canopy overhead.

The street was busy with tourists enjoying the various street entertainers, a wide selection of bars and eateries, and jam-packed casinos. Stockton always preferred the more authentic, vintage Vegas vibe of the downtown area when compared to the modern, extravagant, and overpriced strip.

About halfway down the street, he hung a right and entered the Lasoo Canyon Hotel and Casino, which was among the oldest properties in the city. Built in 1938, the Lasoo was steeped in Vegas history and was seen by many as a relic of the classic era of the city of sin. It had gone through countless renovations over the decades but retained its old-school character and charm. The latest remodeling had gone with a retro art-deco theme and was littered with historical artifacts from the old Mob days. These were displayed throughout the property, making the Lasoo more like a museum hotel.

Stockton enjoyed the unapologetically garish and cheesy glitz of the casino with its low ceilings and dark, smoky, neon-filled atmosphere. It was a cozy old place and seemed to attract a friendlier clientele than most establishments these days. It couldn't be further removed from the self-important opulence of the Baroque Haven.

He had agreed to meet Chambers at the hotel's Risky Neat Lounge at 10:30 a.m. Having arrived early, Stockton decided to pass the time by trying his hand at a quick game of $25 blackjack in the casino. But after eight minutes, Lou, the dealer, had cleaned him out with the speed, skill, and precision of a well-trained Teppanyaki chef cooking Japanese food over an iron griddle.

Never bet on a 6/5 blackjack table, Stockton lamented to himself afterward.

He took a seat at a booth at the Risky Neat and waited for his appointment to show but realized that Chambers was already sitting at the bar. The two men recognized each other from their online photos and found a quiet, darkened corner of the lounge to conduct their meeting. A moment later, a waitress arrived to take their order. Stockton went for a sparkling water while Chambers ordered a scotch. From the smell of the man's breath, Stockton was fairly certain it wasn't his first one of the day.

"I appreciate you agreeing to meet with me on such short notice, Mickey," Stockton said as they took their seats.

"Always glad to help out a fellow flatfoot if I can," Chambers replied.

He was a short, round, and stocky man with a pleasant, jolly face. His wrinkles and floppy grey hair suggested he was roughly in his mid-50s.

"So I won't go through all the details again. I'm trying to get any information I can that helps with finding Eric Dallmeyer's killer. It looks to me like your client, the late Oran Degner, was probably murdered by the same people."

"I'll tell you what I can, but I'll warn you off the bat, Mr. Stockton; if I were you, I'd get off this case as soon as you can and forget about it. The more I've looked into this, the uglier it's gotten. I was no fan of Mr. Degner as a man, but he was clearly killed by powerful people for a reason, and I have no desire to be next."

The man was visibly unnerved. Stockton watched his hand shake as he placed his whiskey glass to his mouth.

"I appreciate the friendly advice. Tell me what you can, and I'll decide for myself if I want to take things further."

Chambers took a mouthful of whiskey and then started talking in a low voice. "Degner wanted me to look into some people for him. He'd done some dealings with a group who'd promised him a big payoff.

Huge money. We're talking hundreds of millions potentially. But it was a con, and he didn't see it coming until it was too late."

Stockton leaned forward in his seat. "What was the nature of this deal?"

"Just over one year ago, an unnamed group approached Degner claiming to be intermediaries for some advertisers. They wanted to install some software on Talaxacorp servers. Some kind of adware virus or somethin'. When a user connects to a Talaxacorp cloud server, the adware would automatically download itself onto their device. Boom! Their personal data is captured and sent back to Talaxacorp. From there, the data was to be sold to advertisers, and Degner would receive a cut."

Stockton was floored. "That's unreal that Degner would agree to such a massive breach of personal user privacy. I know he wasn't exactly the most ethical guy in the world, but this sounds highly illegal and deeply sinister."

Chambers drained his glass. "Trouble is, it was actually so much worse than that, my friend. Degner was the one being conned. Eric Dallmeyer was ordered to install the software on the servers. He was told it was some important security update and was instructed not to look into it too much. About a year passed, so we're up to about two months ago now.

Eric noticed some unusual behavior from the software. He went directly to Degner, and they argued about it. Degner came clean and said it was an adware scam, and he promised to terminate the whole operation if Eric agreed not to go public. The trouble is Eric had looked into it pretty deeply. He discovered that the software was a virus all right, but it wasn't adware after all."

"Interesting. So what did he find?"

Chambers motioned to the waitress for another round.

"I'm not sure, and we might never know if we don't get a good look at Eric's evidence, wherever the hell that is. Eric told Degner something else was going on with the software. Then, one day, Eric showed up at the server room, and it was gone. Poof, into thin air!"

Stockton was confused. "The server room was gone?"

"No, dummy! The software was gone from all the servers! It was like it had never even existed. So Degner wanted to know what these folks had installed on his servers. That's when he hired me to look into them."

"You met Degner at the Baroque Haven a few days before Eric was killed. How did he seem to you?"

"The guy was spooked. But I didn't get the sense

he was worried for his life or anything. More worried about what the scandal could do to his reputation and Talaxacorp. He definitely regretted meeting with those people."

"So who were they?"

"All he gave me was a name, Belinda Goehring. She was the woman who approached him with the deal in the first place."

"What have you got on her?"

"Not a lot, considering it was a fake name. I looked into her entire background, employment history, education, driver's license, social security information, you name it. All forged. This Belinda Goehring persona had been meticulously constructed. That's not an easy thing to do in this day and age where everything's got a digital paper trail. I can think of a few intelligence agencies who have the capability of creating a made-up person like that."

Stockton lightly bit his bottom lip in frustration. "Identifying this woman becomes our highest priority. She could have ordered the hits on Eric and Degner."

The waitress came by with Chambers' drink. He paid her in cash and waited for her to leave before continuing. "Not my priority, kiddo, and it shouldn't be yours either if you know what's good for you. As soon as Eric got iced, I politely told Mr. Degner I was done, and he accepted my withdrawal. End of story.

At least for me. And I highly suggest you end your investigation here, too, pal. It ain't worth losing your head over."

Stockton was silent for a moment as he processed everything he'd heard. "They killed Eric because he knew there was something more going on with their mysterious software. So why kill Degner? What did he know that was so dangerous to these people?"

Chambers watched the ice tinkle in his glass for a moment. "I can't say. Maybe he was just a loose end they wanted to tie up, and when you got involved, they were afraid he'd spill the beans about whoever this mysterious woman was. But like I said, when Eric was killed, I bounced. His death looked staged as hell to me."

Chambers stared at the wall for a moment as something came to his mind. He snapped his fingers. "Oh yeah, before I forget, there was one name that kept coming up when I was doing some digging. A local priest. Briggs, Father Michael Briggs. He seemed to have some connection to Eric."

Stockton took another mouthful of sparkling water, "A priest?"

Chambers shrugged, stood up, and offered Stockton his hand. They shook on it.

"I gotta run. It was a pleasure meeting you, Cody. But like I said, I wouldn't keep pulling on this thread if you want to keep your head. Hey, that rhymes!" He chuckled. "Be safe out there, kiddo."

He turned and left the lounge.

IN THE EARLY AFTERNOON, Stockton grabbed a quick lunch at a burger joint in the Lasoo food hall. While he was on his way out of the casino, he caught sight of a crowd of several dozen people gathered around a bar near the exit. They were all focused on the television in the top right-hand corner of the bar, and Stockton noticed their facial expressions ranged from concern, disbelief, confusion, and shock. His curiosity was sufficiently peaked, and he decided to investigate what the hubbub was all about.

He entered the bar and took a position standing toward the back of the crowd. There was a news broadcast on the TV about a man claiming to be Jesus Christ performing miracles in New York City.

Oh, not this crap again, thought Stockton as he rolled his eyes.

A news reporter on the scene spoke to locals about their experiences. One man claimed that this person, calling himself Jesus, had placed his hand on him and cured his partial blindness. Next, a young woman spoke to the reporter. She described having her cancer cured by this man. Her story was even more extraordinary and included some video evidence.

Stockton and the crowd of onlookers at the bar watched in stunned silence as a short smartphone video clip was played on the news report. The footage was shaky at first but then stabilized. The man claiming to be Jesus sat next to a young bald woman. He placed his hands on either side of the crown of her head. He then removed his hands, and within seconds, her hair began to regrow. The color also returned to her cheeks, and she was overcome with a wave of emotion, breaking down in tears of joy.

A couple of dozen gasps spread throughout the lounge. Stockton paid as much attention to other people's reactions as he did to the news broadcast. A close-up photograph of this Jesus man appeared on the screen. He was Middle Eastern-looking with long brown hair and penetrating blue eyes. Very much what many people envisaged when they thought of the stereotypical image of the Son of God. Even Stockton couldn't deny that the man exuded an intensity and mystery behind his eyes. His consistent message was preaching about the word of God and warning of the grave danger humanity found itself in.

The news anchor explained, "Immigration authorities are at a loss to explain the man's seeming ability to move from one part of the world to the next without any record of going through border checks. He's made appearances on the streets of Sydney, Australia, the Favelas of Rio De Janeiro, and the sprawling metropolis of Singapore, all in a matter of a couple of days. This has led some people to speculate that he must have several doppelgängers. Skeptics have downplayed his supernatural abilities as elaborate illusions and part of some grand hoax."

One journalist who had interviewed Jesus spoke on camera and explained in an incredulous tone, "Jesus believes that mankind has become lazy, decadent, and spiritually bankrupt. He says artificial intelligence cannot be allowed to rule over Mankind and that there can only be one authority in Man's life, God. It's not enough that our mere material needs are met. Our spiritual needs have to be met also. He says that artificial intelligence will be unable to provide for our spiritual sustenance. He has repeatedly stated that under no circumstances should the AI network be reactivated. It must be destroyed."

The news broadcast ended shortly thereafter and went to an ad break. The bartender then hit the mute button on the TV remote control and returned to serving drinks. The crowd took a moment to digest the whole affair, chatting amongst themselves. Stockton was perplexed, not fully knowing what to think. He turned to the man beside him.

"This must be some kind of clever con job."

"No doubt," the man replied. "Probably just a bunch of fancy visual effects, right?"

"Right," agreed Stockton. "I'm just surprised nonsense like this makes the news."

"It looks so real," came a female voice among the crowd.

"Has Jesus really returned?" asked an elderly man.

Stockton stood quietly, listening to the crowd. He saw an older couple with their eyes closed, mouthing prayers in silence.

"It's a miracle!" exclaimed a middle-aged woman seated on a bar stool.

A young man at the back shouted, "I don't believe a second of it."

"How do you explain what you just watched?" replied another man.

"Special effects! CGI!" the young man responded.

A young woman piped up, "My cousin in Mexico witnessed him performing miracles near her town. She sent me a video from her phone. It's real! Jesus has returned!"

She held up her phone and began playing the video clip. Some of the crowd began gathering around her to watch it.

Stockton rolled his eyes and shook his head.

"Mass hysteria," he muttered under his breath. He'd seen enough and decided to leave the bar.

Some people can't help but get caught up in the latest social media clickbait rubbish.

HE TOOK a contemplative stroll back to his apartment and decided to spend the afternoon writing up his case notes and conducting research. He grabbed some reheated coffee from the kitchen, then returned to his office and switched on his computer. While he waited for the practically antique PC to boot up, he sipped his cup of joe and stared out the window at the passing downtown street traffic.

Chambers had warned him to drop the case and walk away, and the man certainly had good reason. His billionaire client had been murdered by the same forces who'd killed Eric Dallmeyer. If they were capable of such extreme actions, what hope did a man like Stockton have? He knew he was in way over his head. Continuing any further with his investigation looked increasingly like a one-way trip to the morgue.

During the war, he'd accepted overwhelming odds countless times. He'd found the prospect of death preferable to living as an AI-controlled slave.

As a result, he became conditioned to prioritize the mission over his well-being.

As far as he was concerned, evil was evil; it existed to be fought, no matter the cost. He wasn't even entirely sure what was driving him forward and compelling him to solve this case, but the more the danger increased, so too did his determination.

Despite Chambers' warnings, walking away from a fight simply wasn't in his nature. Throughout his life, he'd often faced his biggest challenges alone.

His mind drifted back to the news report from earlier. He was astounded at the gullibility of some people to believe in such obvious hoaxes. *Maybe they need to believe?* he considered.

He sometimes envied those who could call upon their faith in God to spiritually fortify them in times of great adversity. There was a time when he sought such comfort from a higher power, but that was before the war had utterly broken him.

He'd long ago given up on the idea of a messiah riding over the hill on a white horse. The bloodshed, carnage, and destruction Stockton had witnessed during the war had hardened his heart to comforting notions like God, divine justice, and the afterlife.

As much as a small part of him might still have wanted to believe, the death, misery, and destruction he'd observed obliterated his innocence and crushed his faith. Sometimes, he didn't know how Zara could put up with his cynicism.

His computer finally finished booting, and he slumped into his desk and logged in. His brief meeting with Chambers had at least proved somewhat fruitful. He'd gotten a name that might provide more insights and advance his case. He typed into a search engine: *Father Michael Briggs*. Apparently, he was a local parish priest who knew Eric Dallmeyer. It sounded like another promising lead.

CHAPTER
SEVEN

THE NEXT DAY, Stockton made the 35-minute drive north on route 95 to Father Briggs' home at 11920 Saint Luke's Avenue in Indian Springs.

Briggs had seemed eager to talk with Stockton. He had known Eric Dallmeyer personally and had been devastated by the news of his untimely death.

Briggs greeted him at the front door of his small bungalow with a warm smile and a firm handshake. The elderly man wore a dark grey cardigan over a black shirt, with black trousers. He was roughly five-foot-eight, and from the lines on his face and thick white hair on his head, he was probably pushing 70, or near enough.

He led Stockton into his sparsely decorated dining room, where he had already prepared the table with plates, a tray of sandwiches, and a pot of coffee. Stockton found the whole effort unnecessarily generous. The level of care and wholesomeness reminded him of visiting his grandmother as a young boy.

"Father, this is too much. You didn't have to go to all of this trouble," said Stockton appreciatively.

"Not at all. I assure you it was nothing, really. The sandwiches were made by the ladies from the parish hall. They were leftovers from one of our recent gatherings. Please, take a seat and help yourself."

Stockton pulled out one of the hardwood table chairs and sat down. "Where's your parish church, Father?"

Briggs sat opposite him and poured out their coffees. "Saint Sanela's. Do you know it?"

"I've heard of it, though I'm not a churchgoer myself. My girlfriend attends mass there." Stockton blew steam off the top of his mug and took a quiet slurp of coffee. "Have you been working at this parish long?"

Briggs smiled. "Thirteen months now. I arrived here last March." He paused for a moment and tried to remember the exact date. "It was March 24th, if memory serves. I work alongside Father Phillips. Your girlfriend probably knows him."

"She's mentioned him before." Stockton placed his mug on the table. "So, as I explained over the phone, my client's name is Olivia. She's the sister of the late Eric Dallmeyer. You said you knew him?"

The muscles in Briggs' face tightened slightly as if the very mention of Eric's name was painful to him. He nodded solemnly. "Awful, just awful. What horrific fate befell that wonderful young man. Such a courageous soul."

"Can you tell me how the two of you met?"

"He came to a prayer meeting a few months ago. I found him to be a courteous young man but quiet and clearly distracted by something. He was carrying a great burden on his shoulders, that much was certain. The weight of the world, it seemed. He took me to one side after the meeting; he needed a friend, someone to confide in."

Stockton reached for a triangular cheese and ham sandwich from the tray in front of him. "I take it that Eric spoke to you about his work?"

Briggs wrapped his two hands around his coffee mug.

"He told me he was facing some, what's the word? *Intimidation* from outside forces. Eric explained to me that he had identified what he described as an anomaly in the computer systems in his workplace. Something that shouldn't have been there. He threatened to take the matter to a local radio station and a popular news website. Of course, his boss told him not to do it."

Briggs' eyes stared downward for a moment as the wheels turned in his mind. "We met privately twice, no, three times. We prayed together for strength and protection."

Stockton nodded while chewing his sandwich. "I understand. You mentioned Eric had faced some intimidation. Can you explain more about that?"

"Yes, there had been strange phone calls in the middle of the night. He'd answer the phone, but the line would go dead. His home was broken into while he was away. One day, he came home and found that his furniture had been moved around. Nothing was damaged. Nothing was stolen. There was no sign of a break-in. It was all designed to make him paranoid, to scare him. To show him that they could come and go as they pleased. Then there were the symbols."

Stockton sat forward. "Symbols?"

Briggs removed a sheet of paper from the left breast pocket of his shirt. He unfolded it and laid it on the table. Stockton looked it over closely. The symbol resembled a kind of pentagram with an S-like icon at the center of it.

Briggs continued. "The symbol was scrawled in graffiti on a wall near his home. Then, sometime later, it was etched into the bodywork of his car."

Stockton considered for a moment how Olivia had never mentioned any of this level of detail when he spoke with her. It was clear that Eric had confided a great deal more in Father Briggs than he had in his sister.

"Do you recognize the symbol?"

"As a matter of fact, I do, and it's the reason I said so many decades of the rosary for Eric. He had unwittingly stumbled onto the radar of a wicked and malevolent cult."

Stockton raised an eyebrow. "A cult? You're saying a cult is behind Eric's death?"

A cult? he thought to himself. *I didn't see that coming. This changes everything.*

Briggs nodded thoughtfully. "A parishioner of mine is a former member. I helped him rediscover Jesus and come back to the faith. His name is Daniel Serk. When I'd informed him of the symbols, he immediately wanted to speak to Eric, but it was too late. Eric died before the two men ever met."

Briggs placed an elbow on the table and his forehead in his hand. "I failed him, Cody. It was my duty as his spiritual leader to protect him. My only solace is that I know his soul has found its way to our Lord."

Stockton studied the old man's despondent face for a moment. "I'm not sure there's much you could have done, Father. Eric's killers seem quite sophisticated, not to mention dangerous. But I have to say, I'm a little taken aback by what you've told me. I'd presumed whoever killed Eric had been trying to cover up some kind of money-making scam being run at Talaxacorp. But if a *cult* is behind all of this, then their motivation may not be financial, but ideological instead."

Stockton reflected on this for a moment, playing with his mustache and realizing he'd seriously underestimated the perpetrators. "What can you tell me about this cult?"

"Daniel Serk is the man you need to speak with now. He can give you all of the details. But unfortunately, I cannot reach him anymore. A few days after Eric died, Daniel stopped taking my calls. His phone was disconnected, and I'm unable to contact him."

A weariness and concern swept across Briggs' face. "I went to his home several times. I even phoned the police to report him missing. They've been unable to locate him. I'm terribly worried that the cult may have murdered him."

Stockton wiped some mayonnaise from his mouth with a table napkin. "Do you remember how he seemed the last time you spoke with him? Did he give you any indication that he was in danger?"

"The last correspondence I have from Daniel was an email he sent a day or two after Eric was found dead."

"Can you show me this email?"

"I can indeed," said Briggs, reaching for his smartphone, which was lying on a newspaper on the far side of the table.

He swiped, tapped, and scrolled on the display

for several moments and then handed the device to Stockton with the email open on the screen. Stockton read the message quietly:

Father,

I'm truly broken by this news and appalled by their cruelty and malice. However, I'm not surprised at the desperation of their actions. Eric was a brave man and a champion for truth. God will make them pay for what they've done. The Lord will never allow them to prevail.

What should I do now? I can't let them find me. Perhaps if we consider things carefully, hidden beneath, we can discern my place in all of this. I firmly believe nothing that we do, is done in vain. I believe, with all my soul, that we shall see the triumph.

Before we know the truth, we must first be able to see it.

God bless you, Father,

Daniel

"And that's all he sent you?" Stockton asked.

"Yes, that's everything. What do you think?"

Stockton reached into his trouser pocket, removed his phone, and proceeded to take a photograph of the email on Briggs' device before returning it to the old man.

"It sounds to me like he was terrified for his own life. Do you think it's possible he went into hiding?"

"I sincerely hope so. I've prayed for him night and day these past six weeks. If you can track him down, Cody, he'll provide all the information about the cult."

Stockton drank some more coffee. "I'll see what I can do, In the meantime, is there anything you can tell me about them? What do they want?"

"I can tell you that they worship Satan," said Briggs. "They've existed for many hundreds of years, and in most recent times, they've taken a keen interest in technology as a means of contacting the devil."

Stockton's eyes grew wide. "The devil? Seriously?"

This is definitely not some money-making scam.

"Do you think this cult installed something on the Talaxacorp servers that had something to do with contacting Satan?"

Briggs stared intently into Stockton's eyes.

"Cody, I have no doubt."

Stockton was incredulous. "How would a computer virus spread across millions of devices help a cult speak with the devil? This all sounds absurd to me."

"Daniel can fill you in on the intricate details of their plan. He was a fairly high-up member and privy to a significant amount of their inner workings.

He also knows what they're planning to do next. And they're planning to do it soon."

"I presume you're aware that it's likely this cult is also responsible for the murder of Oran Degner?"

Briggs nodded.

Stockton looked at Briggs, slightly askew.

"So, if you suspected this cult was responsible for Eric's death back when it happened, why didn't you contact the police and notify them?"

"And have the police chasing phantoms who have infiltrated key positions of authority in our state institutions? What would be the point? Moreover, notifying the police would simply place many more people in grave danger. The police officers themselves would quickly face the wrath of the cult, and to be frank, Cody, this isn't a fight for mere mortals."

"I'm sorry, I'm confused, Father. Two men have been murdered, and if you have any idea as to where we can find the perpetrators…"

Briggs raised a hand and interrupted him.

"This is a spiritual battle, Cody. This is not a concern of the quaint laws of Man. This is a time of great tribulation and turmoil. Heaven and Hell are pitted in a titanic battle together, and humanity must choose the side of God because, in the end, God wins. This cult can only be defeated by Jesus Christ."

Stockton pursed his lips and grimaced slightly. Though Father Briggs seemed like a pleasant and affable old man, to Stockton, this all sounded like the zealous and delusional ramblings of a religious nutcase.

"Father, with all due respect, your religious beliefs and convictions are your own business. Your spiritual interpretation of events is not of any concern to me or the law. Myself and the police are trying to track down murderers here. If you truly knew where to find them, you'd be doing your friend Eric Dallmeyer a great disservice by refusing to supply useful information that could lead to their whereabouts and arrest."

Briggs took a moment to reply. "But what can I do now, Cody? Daniel Serk has disappeared, after all."

"And I'll do what I can to locate him," Stockton replied more calmly.

"But I can assure you, Cody, the cult can only be stopped by the Son of God, and he has returned to fulfill that very purpose."

Stockton's head cocked to the side slightly.

"Wait, hold on a second. What are you saying here? Do you believe this guy who's all over the news right now, claiming to be Jesus, is the real deal?"

Briggs smiled widely. "I do."

Stockton was taken aback and tittered uncomfortably to himself. "Well, personally, I don't buy any of it for a second. The whole story smacks of a clever hoax to me. I haven't figured out what the purpose of it is just yet, but I'm sure it'll become clear soon enough."

Briggs studied Stockton's face and responded thoughtfully. "I know we've only just met, but I've been told I'm a good judge of character." He gestured with his hands again. "I can evaluate a person on a spiritual level quite quickly, and I see within you a great capacity for faith."

Stockton sat back in his chair and chuckled.

"Well, no offense, but I think your faith radar might need recalibration because I am certainly not a man of faith."

Briggs grinned. "But you used to be, yes?"

"I used to be, that's correct. It might even surprise you to know that I studied theology for several years with a view to becoming a pastor. So I'm fairly well versed in the Bible, at least for a layman."

"Do you mind telling me what transpired that made you slip away from God's word?"

"I went into the war a believer, with a strong sense that God was on our side. I came out of the war convinced that he was nothing more than a trick of the mind. A coping mechanism to help make sense of a senseless world. There's no way a loving God could allow the horror and pain I witnessed."

Briggs refilled their coffee mugs. "God has permitted man to make all manner of calamitous mistakes for several hundred years for an important reason."

"Let me guess." Stockton interrupted with a sarcastic grin. "To teach us some kind of a lesson, right? Suffering strengthens our faith in God or some other such baloney?"

"While it is true that enduring suffering can bring us closer to God, suffering on this Earth is only made possible by Man failing to obey God's laws and misusing his free will."

Stockton leaned back in his chair. "It seems that God has no problem standing idly by forever, watching humanity unnecessarily suffer horror after horror, which he could so easily have prevented with the wave of his hand."

Briggs raised a finger. "Cody, you misunderstand. For centuries now, God stepped back and chose not to intervene in this fallen realm. He permitted Man to forge his own path. And look where it's taken us. Man has rejected the transcendent in favor of the material, frivolous, and carnal."

He wiped away some crumbs from his sleeve and continued. "A few years ago, foolish men thought that they could emulate God's power with the omnipresent and total authority of artificial intelligence. The outcome was yet more years of anguish and suffering. But we're fortunate to have had men like yourself. Men of character and courage. Whether you realize it or not, whether you intended it or not, fighting for the emancipation of mankind during the war was a contribution to God's work."

Stockton shrugged nonchalantly. "I still maintain that if God chose to, he could have prevented the AI from being built in the first place."

"And through you, he demonstrated his will and his grace. Whether you believe in our Lord or not, Cody, to do good is to be of God."

Stockton shook his head in dismay. "Not that it did us much good in the end. If the clowns in charge of the world have their way, this time next week, it looks like we're about to make the same mistake all over again. The AI is coming back, and there are scarcely enough strong young men left to stop it this time."

"No, I'm certain the AI will be stopped," Briggs replied with a steely confidence in his voice. "The Lord has seen enough. He's about to show his hand in the manner you have so desperately longed for. Alas, in such a world of doubt and cynicism, there will be those who will refuse to believe their own eyes. Even the extraordinary miracles Jesus will perform will not convince them."

"I hate to disappoint you." Stockton's mouth curled into a grin. "I'm probably one of those skeptics you're talking about."

Briggs gestured with both hands. "Cody, proof of

God's existence is and always has been all around us. It's hardcoded into the very essence of our reality for those who have eyes to see it."

Stockton placed his palms on the table and prepared to leave. "Well, if God does show his face, he's going to get an earful from me, I can tell you."

He stood up from his chair. "On that note, Father, I'll thank you for your hospitality. I've enjoyed our conversation. Very nice to meet you." He offered the old man his hand, which Briggs shook tightly.

"I wish you the very best of luck locating Daniel. You let me know when you've found him, won't you?"

"Of course, Father, and if there's any other useful information you can think of, you have my number."

Briggs led Stockton down the hallway and opened the front door. The two men stood in the doorway for a moment.

"If there's anything else I can help you with, or if you simply need some spiritual guidance, don't hesitate to stop by," Briggs beamed.

"I think my girlfriend would very much enjoy speaking with you. She's devoutly Christian."

"Oh, by all means. Tell her my door is always open."

"She's always trying to get me to go to confession."

"I suspect if you listen to her, Cody, she'll help lead you to the truth."

"Good day, Father."

Stockton strode back down the driveway towards his car. A moment later, as he started the engine and slowly pulled away from the curb, he was satisfied that despite all of the religious claptrap, his visit to Father Briggs had at least been constructive. He now knew that a cult had been behind the deaths of Dallmeyer and Degner. He just had to hope that one of its former members—Daniel Serk—was still alive.

Regardless, learning that a Satan-worshiping cult was behind the murders disturbed him greatly and radically altered the complexion of the case. As Stockton reached the onramp for the highway, the weight of this revelation finally hit him.

Throughout his career, he'd come face to face with the ugliest aspects of human nature. In his experience, the typical justifications that motivated someone to commit murder were hatred, money, sex, power, and revenge. But the motivations of a cult were an entirely different matter. They were based on ideology and firmly held convictions, no matter how twisted. People of such belief systems were more likely to go to extremes to accomplish their goals. This made them a far more dangerous adversary. Mickey Chambers' warnings began to echo louder in his head.

CHAPTER
EIGHT

IT HAD BEEN a long time since Stockton could remember having such a vivid dream. As the intrusive beeping of his alarm clock yanked him back to the land of consciousness, he lay in bed recalling a jumble of letters and numbers dancing in his field of view. He'd seen what looked like several words obscured behind frosted glass.

He sat up and tapped the button on the alarm clock, yawned, stretched, and tried to recall what he'd seen before the memory of his dream faded. He felt certain that, for just a moment, there had been some significance or meaning to the letters and numbers, as if he'd briefly understood something that was now lost to him. He could just about recall seeing the number six and the letters A, B, and E.

Abe? A person's name, perhaps? He didn't know anyone by that name.

After a long, high-pressure shower, he dried himself and got dressed but noticed he could hear voices coming from down the hall. He entered the living room and saw that Zara had let herself into the apartment and was lying on the couch, staring at the television.

"Hey," she said absentmindedly, without turning to look at him. She sounded like she was very much engrossed in the news report.

"Hey," Stockton replied, rubbing his wet hair with the towel. "What's going on?"

"There's huge riots happening all over the place. Check it out." She raised the volume on the TV remote control.

The news report showed violent clashes between anti-AI protesters and riot police on the streets of several US cities such as Dallas, New York, Chicago, Baltimore, Los Angeles, Kansas, Washington DC, Jacksonville, Milwaukee, and Atlanta.

Significant property damage had been done in the downtown areas of those cities, including shop looting and buildings and vehicles being set on fire. At least one hundred people had been arrested, and dozens injured.

The protesters had demanded that the US government and the international community dismantle the AI node network immediately, which was due to be reactivated in four days.

"And look at this," said Zara, changing the channel with the remote.

Another news channel was running a story about how Jesus Christ was now in Berlin, Germany, and speaking to an enthusiastic crowd of over one million people at the steps of the Reichstag building. He demanded that world leaders obey God's command and abandon the artificial intelligence network at once.

The report also included other clips of Jesus forgiving sins and healing the sick and dying in hospitals across the world. He did this by simply placing his hands on them. They appeared to miraculously recover from their ailments almost immediately.

Some witnesses who spoke to Jesus claimed that he not only knew their names but also knew very intimate details about their lives.

Zara pressed a button on the remote and switched to another news station. "It's on every channel," she gasped.

The next news report showed a clip of Jesus being mobbed by an enormous crowd in Bucharest, Romania, from three days earlier. The shaky camera zoomed back to a wide shot, and a flash of yellow light could be seen from within the sea of people. The crowd reacted vocally in shock and confusion. Then, there was another flash of yellow light several hundred yards away. The camera panned to the left and above to show that Jesus was now standing alone on the top of a building, looking down at the crowd.

"That's a neat trick," said Stockton. "I've seen a lot of good magic shows in Vegas, but that one was smoothly done."

Another broadcast showed Jesus preaching and conducting baptisms to a crowd of millions on a stage in Venice, Italy. The gathering was from the previous day. After he was finished, he stepped away from the podium, turned to his right, and an ovular halo of light shimmered into view in midair. It was roughly seven feet tall, four feet wide, and only a few inches in depth. It hung in the air for several seconds. Jesus stepped into this "portal" and then disappeared. The halo shimmered momentarily and vanished.

Zara was transfixed and anxiously rubbed the crucifix around her neck. "So that's how he's able to travel all over the world instantly."

Stockton placed the towel around his neck and took a seat on the arm of the couch. He studied the screen in utter disbelief.

Zara continued, "They say there's been two attempts on his life already. Someone in Columbia tried to shoot him, and the bullet just bounced off."

Stockton looked at her with a troubled expression.

He crossed the living room to the television and switched it off.

"What did you do that for?" she asked.

"This is… I don't know what this is, Zara, but it's got to be some kind of hoax. It's like the world has gone insane or something. There has to be a logical and rational explanation for all this."

"Yeah, there is," she replied. "But you don't want to hear it, Cody. Maybe what's happening is real, and your pride won't let you accept it."

He placed his hands on his hips and stared at the floor, trying to make sense of what he'd just seen. A tense silence filled the air for a moment.

He picked up his phone from the cabinet beneath the TV and checked the time. He noticed there was a message notification. It was from eleven hours earlier. He swiped and tapped to reveal it was from his younger brother, Marcus, who lived in Australia with his wife, Audrey. Marcus had uploaded a short video he'd filmed on his phone with the following text attached: "We took Mom to see Jesus when he visited Canberra this week, and look what happened next."

Stockton tapped the play button on the video. It showed Audrey's mother, Joyce, seated in her wheelchair on stage with Jesus in a closed-off area of the city. A crowd of several thousand had gathered to watch.

"Zara," Stockton's voice trembled. "Come look at this."

She jumped up from the couch and stood next to him. They stared at the smartphone screen together.

"Who is that?" she asked him.

"That's Joyce, Audrey's mother, you remember? I told you about her. She had her right leg amputated from the knee down a few years back. Infection set in after she'd been in a car accident."

The video clip showed Jesus placing his hands on Joyce's thigh. Marcus zoomed in on the amputated leg, and within seconds, what appeared to be a few small toes began to emerge from the knee stump. The toes continued to grow outward, followed by a foot and then an ankle, and then the shin and calf until the entire right leg was fully restored. The process was completed in less than twenty seconds.

Stockton and Zara looked at each other aghast. She placed both hands over her mouth, her eyes as wide as dinner plates, her face white as a sheet. Stockton's mind scrambled for a rational explanation, but none was forthcoming.

They watched in disbelief as the video continued. The crowd erupted into applause and euphoric cheering. Joyce embraced Jesus and wept tears of joy. The footage began to shake slightly as Marcus could be heard crying from behind his phone.

Jesus helped her to her feet, and she stood and

walked unaided for the first time in five years. The crowd grew louder. Marcus turned the camera to face Audrey to his right. She was covering her mouth and sobbing.

Stockton's blood ran cold, and his heart was racing. *What the hell is going on?*

He swiped down further. Marcus had uploaded more footage and photos of a smiling and now fully able-bodied Joyce. The last post was a short audio clip from Marcus. Stockton tapped the play button.

"Cody, can you believe this?" Marcus had to shout to be heard over the crowd noise. "Did you watch the video? She's healed! Joyce is healed! Praise be to the Lord Jesus Christ!"

These were words Stockton never expected to hear from his brother, who had been a hardcore atheist for as long as he'd known him.

"We love you, big bro! We can't wait to see you when we get back to the States this fall. God bless you and Zara. Call us when you get this. We'll stay up late tonight…" The audio recording stopped.

Stockton stood staring in silence at the phone for several minutes and then looked at Zara, still covering her mouth, tears were quietly sliding down her cheeks. He then replayed the video of Joyce's regrown leg; they rewatched it together.

"How do you explain that?" Zara asked, her voice wavering.

The video finished playing, and he looked at her. "I can't."

A FLURRY of news reports continued pouring in for the rest of the day. Zara remained glued to the television, channel surfing and watching media analysis, videos, and testimonials about Jesus' miracles and his various public statements. Stockton struggled to concentrate on anything important and retreated to his office to update his case notes on his computer. He kept his office door open and listened to the TV news coverage coming from the living room.

As he typed away at his keyboard, he overheard the voice of a former senior advisor to the US President discussing a rumor about how the White House will soon announce the demolition of the US Node of the AI network.

Another source claimed that Jesus had gathered several world leaders together, transported them to an undisclosed location, and instructed them to destroy the AI nodes as soon as possible. Allegedly, Jesus wanted humans to destroy the AI network themselves rather than have him do it. He wished to give them the opportunity to intentionally choose God as the primary authority in their lives and not the AI system. Another report stated that Jesus had gathered some of the world's richest people together and convinced them to donate huge portions of their wealth to feed the poor and starving.

In the late evening, Zara left the apartment for about an hour and grabbed some takeout dinners from a local Chinese restaurant. She and Stockton ate together in his office. He sat behind his desk while she sat opposite him in one of the client chairs.

"I'm exhausted," she said as she picked her way through her box of chicken noodle stir fry with a pair of chopsticks.

"I know the feeling," Stockton chewed a mouthful of fried vegetables as he spoke. "It's more emotionally draining than anything, you know? I thought I could find a rational explanation for everything. The world just seems to be getting stranger and stranger every day. Of course, I'm not discounting the possibility that the head injury I suffered a few days ago could have put me in a coma, and this is all just a bizarre dream."

Zara half-smiled and popped a goujon in her mouth.

After she finished chewing, she asked, "If you met Jesus, what would you ask him?"

Stockton loaded up his fork with some onions and a jumbo shrimp and took a bite.

"Oh, I don't know, maybe, where have you been

for the past two thousand years? Where were you when the Roman Empire fell or during the Bubonic plague? Why didn't you intervene and stop the First and Second World Wars from happening? Why didn't you come back and stop the AI War? Why did you decide to come back now? And those would be just off the top of my head."

"I get it, babe. I understand your frustration, but he must have his reasons," Zara replied. "Father Philips says God stood back for a few centuries and let us mess up a bunch. He took the training wheels off so that we'd figure out we couldn't go it alone and that we needed him. I guess he's proven his point."

"Yeah, Father Briggs believes the same thing." He took a sip from his can of soda. "Well, obviously, I'm ecstatic that the AI node network is being destroyed at least. But it doesn't let God off the hook for not stepping in when he could have."

"Cody, it doesn't matter now," Zara said, putting her takeout box on the table. "He's here *now*, that's what's important. Believers are vindicated in their faith, and nonbelievers now know the truth. When I went outside earlier, I could sense this incredible energy from people, you know? There's this kind of infectious joy and excitement on the streets. It's like people have a new meaning in their lives."

Stockton sat forward, placing his elbows on his

desk. He closed his eyes and rubbed his temples. "I swear this is one helluva coma," he whispered.

Zara giggled. "'Fraid not, soldier. I'm as real as it gets. Come and touch me if you don't believe me." She gave him a smoldering look and then a suggestive pout.

An awkward smile crossed his lips. He leaned back in his chair. "If the whole God thing turns out to be true, doesn't it make you feel kinda small? Sort of insignificant?"

Her brow wrinkled slightly. "Not me. If anything, it makes me feel the opposite, like I'm connected to something much bigger than myself. It's comforting."

He wiped the corner of his mouth with a napkin. "I dunno. The idea of a higher power governing the universe just makes me feel like there's things beyond Man's control. I find that hard to accept. I can tell you if I met Jesus right now, he could probably tell me where I could find Daniel Serk."

"This is the guy from the cult?"

"Yep, Father Briggs texted me a photo of him earlier. Young guy, maybe in his late-twenties, with blond hair and medium build. I searched online and found a handful of Daniel Serks, but none of them matched the guy in the photo. It's like he has zero social media presence. I called Ridgemore while you were glued to the TV. He says Serk was officially reported missing five days after Eric Dallmeyer was killed."

Zara's expression turned grim. "You think the cult may have killed him?"

"It's possible, but I have a feeling he's still alive. Call it a hunch, but there's something about the esoteric nature of his final email to Briggs that leads me to believe he *may* have tried to go underground."

Stockton handed her his phone with the photo of the email on display.

Zara read the words quietly. "I don't see anything strange in that email. Sounds like he was worried they were going to come after him next."

Stockton stroked his mustache and fixed a thoughtful gaze on Zara. "Read the second paragraph again."

Zara read it aloud this time.

What should I do now? I can't let them find me. Perhaps if we consider things carefully, hidden beneath, we can discern my place in all of this. I firmly believe nothing that we do, is done in vain. I believe, with all my soul, that we shall see the triumph. Before we know the truth, we must first be able to see it.

She shrugged and handed the phone back to him.

Stockton pressed his lips together thoughtfully. "I think there's something buried in there, something he wanted Father Briggs to find."

Zara tilted her head to the side. "What? You mean like a code or something?"

"Exactly. Don't you think there's something kind of odd about the wording he used?"

"Maybe he was just trying to sound fancy?" Zara replied. "But I'll admit, it almost sounds familiar."

"Like, it could be a literary quote from something?"

"Maybe. It does sound a bit too theatrical for such a serious email."

Stockton opened a web browser on his PC and navigated to a search engine. He typed out the entire second paragraph of the email into the search box and hit enter. A moment later, a page full of results popped up. Several of them highlighted the line in question: *I firmly believe nothing that we do, is done in vain. I believe, with all my soul, that we shall see the triumph.*

As Stockton had suspected, the text was identified as a literary quote.

"I knew it," he said, scrolling through the relevant results. "It says here it's a line from *A Tale of Two Cities* by Charles Dickens from 1859."

"I thought it sounded kind of familiar," Zara got up and walked around his desk to take a look at the screen. She placed a hand on his shoulder and gently leaned close to him.

"Maybe he just likes to include appropriate

quotes from his favorite books in his emails?" she suggested.

Stockton's forehead creased a little as he frowned in disagreement. "Maybe, but I don't think so. Look at the final line after the quote."

He read it to her aloud. "'Before we know the truth, we must first be able to see it.' That particular line sounds like a clue to me. He wanted Father Briggs to see something. Check out the line before the quote. 'Perhaps if we consider things carefully, hidden beneath, we can discern my place in all of this.' Now, that sounds like a dead giveaway. He wants Briggs to consider the content of the email more carefully. He's telling him that there's something hidden beneath the message."

"And it's something to do with the Dickens quote?" Zara asked.

"Exactly." Stockton pointed a finger at the screen. "And I think I know what it relates to. Serk says, 'We can discern my place in all of this.' What if there's a double meaning there?"

He re-read the line once more. "The word 'place' might not just mean his place in the situation metaphorically but his *place* literally. As in, his location."

"Hmm, you might be onto something, babe. Pull up the quote from Dickens again."

Stockton clicked his mouse back onto a search

result about *A Tale of Two Cities*. They both read the quote again quietly.

"I just did a quick scan of the first letters of every word. I'm not seeing any obvious abbreviations. Maybe the code is much simpler than that."

Stockton mulled it over. "This book has been in the public domain for a long time. There's probably been a ton of reprints, abridged versions, and unabridged versions. So, the code is unlikely to involve page numbers because the number of pages in the book would vary from one reprint to another. That means the code has to relate to things that remain consistent. Title, chapters, characters…"

"Books," Zara added.

"Books?"

"Yes, books," she replied. "*A Tale of Two Cities* is told across three books."

"Oh. I didn't know that."

"You haven't read *A Tale of Two Cities*?"

"Nope."

She looked at him, surprised. "Cody, for a man well-read in theology, you sure haven't read a lot of classics."

"I know, I know. *A Tale of Two Cities* is up there with *War and Peace*, *Moby Dick* and *Ulysses*. Books they say you're supposed to read at some point in your life, but I can just never seem to find the time.

Mind you, the first chapter of *Ulysses* was one chapter too many."

He took out a pen and paper from the top drawer of his desk and prepared to write something down. "Which book does the quote appear in?"

Zara tried to recall. "I don't remember off hand."

Stockton tapped and clicked away at his computer a few more times. "There it is. Book two, chapter 16. Maybe the code is literally that simple. Although we could be going about this the wrong way entirely."

Zara took the pen and scribbled on the paper: *B2C16.*

Stockton typed it into the search engine. He puffed out his cheeks in frustration. "Nothing relevant from these search results."

He paused, his eyes growing larger.

Unless. It does look a lot like a postcode.

The combination of letters and numbers resembled one of those new postcodes that the AI had introduced ten years earlier to streamline its tracking capabilities. The old US zip code service had been retired in half the country and replaced with a more efficient postal address sorting system.

He brought up a postcode finder website and entered B2C16. A moment later, the screen returned an address.

1171 East Denver Avenue, Bravery, Nevada.

"Well, what do you know?" He grinned widely and turned to look into Zara's gorgeous green eyes. Her mouth was wide open with giddy excitement.

He studied the location using an online mapping service.

"That's about a three-hour drive from here." He rubbed his hands together and then cracked his knuckles, feeling justifiably pleased with himself. "Daniel Serk, consider yourself located."

"Oh, you are very clever, aren't you?" Zara bit her bottom lip. Her voice became low and sultry. "Did anyone ever tell you you could make a pretty good detective?"

"Why thank you," he said, grabbing her by the waist and pulling her down onto his lap. She squealed with delight and then kissed him fervently.

He smiled suggestively. "You know I've been looking for an assistant to help me with some… how do I say this? U*ndercover* work, if you're interested?"

She threw her head back and chuckled. "Smooth, Mr. Detective, very smooth."

CHAPTER
NINE

HE ENTERED the postcode into his car's GPS and hit the road just before noon. Stockton had never visited Bravery before. It was an old mining town founded in 1897 and known for its snowy winters and dry, hot summers.

He took the Extraterrestrial Highway, passing by a plethora of UFO-themed hotels, motels, diners, and kitschy monuments to little green men. Regular signage along the highway provided constant reminders of cheesy local attractions about UFO sightings and museums dedicated to all things otherworldly. A veritable sacred land for UFO conspiracy nuts.

Stockton smiled. He never bought into any of it himself, but he figured it formed part of the local folklore, offering an opportunity to build a tourist industry that appeared moderately lucrative. He considered how redundant the idea of alien visitors seemed, considering the son of the creator of the universe himself was now walking the Earth—or at least that's how it appeared. He still didn't know what to believe, and yet the evidence was highly convincing. Christ's return certainly put everything into perspective.

Unlike these alleged UFO encounters, of which there was little to no tangible proof, Christ was now seemingly flesh and blood and performing miracles left, right, and center. Little green alien visitors from another planet seemed pretty insignificant when stacked up against the return of the Almighty.

As he drove with the top down through the desert air, he considered the remoteness and desolation of this whole desert region. There was a unique atmosphere about it that he had always liked, a romanticism about the place. Though the true cowboys were long gone and the gold veins had dried up, the ghosts of prospectors and adventurers still lingered in the canyons, valleys, and mountain ranges of the region.

The pioneering energy of the 19th-century frontier never fully left this part of the world. It had largely maintained the inescapable excitement that comes with living on the edge of the wild and untamed. This was a proving ground for the indomitable human spirit. There was a sense that you were far enough away from the interference of authorities and could be left alone to enjoy your freedom.

Humanity had lost such ideals at the beginning of the 21st century, but after the war, most people had rapidly begun to rediscover them once again. These were good times to live in, even if most people were less well-off. At least they were more free, and so long as the AI didn't succeed in taking over the world, that freedom would endure.

In places like this, the idea of a looming dark shadow of technological authoritarianism seemed lightyears away.

EVIDENCE of the post-war economic collapse was hard to ignore in the sleepy town of Bravery. As Stockton cruised through the main street, he was overwhelmed by the sheer number of boarded-up shop fronts with 'out of business' signs in the windows. The town had decayed badly in recent years, and most of its young people had left to seek opportunities elsewhere. The city's remaining businesses tried desperately to attract passing trade from motorists driving between

Vegas and Reno, which Bravery was about halfway between.

In Stockton's opinion, Serk had chosen an ideal location as a hideaway. Few people would ever think to look for a person in a forgotten town like Bravery.

He drove beyond the downtown area and, about five minutes later, was on the outskirts of town heading towards a dusty caravan park. This was home to the town's mostly elderly population, who lived in dilapidated shacks and mobile homes.

The GPS directed him to the most extreme north end of the park, along a winding, dusty, dirt track road until he reached a rickety picket fence at the edge of a remote farmhouse.

He parked his car beside the silver letter box, which contained the postcode B2C16 stenciled on the side. It took him about three minutes to walk the long driveway to the house.

From a distance, the simple two-story timber building looked like a derelict. The exterior timber frame was showing considerable signs of rot and termite damage. Several windows were cracked, though not broken, and the roof looked to be in rough shape.

Stockton considered just how safe Serk was living in a place like this.

If the cult doesn't kill him, the building might just do the job by collapsing on top of him at a moment's notice.

The house sat on several dozen acres of unused farmland and was surrounded by three outbuildings, including some sheds. One of them was a small well house that supplied the property with water.

He stepped up onto the creaking wooden porch, being cautious not to put his foot through a compromised floorboard. He peered through one of the filthy ground-floor windows, wiping away some cobwebs to get a better look inside.

The interior of the house looked about as uninhabitable as the exterior suggested. However, despite the kitchen and dining area looking fairly unsightly, Stockton was pleased to see it had been used recently. What looked like a brand-new gas cylinder and camping stove sat next to a foldout aluminum table, on top of which lay a few used plastic cups, plates, and kitchen utensils. The remnants of a recently eaten meal.

Stockton turned to his left towards the front door and prepared to knock on it. Until the sound of a gun cock froze his blood to his bones.

"Not another move, or I'll shoot," said a shaky voice from behind him.

Stockton instinctively threw his arms in the air.

"Uh-huh. Turn around slowly. Nice and easy. Don't reach for anything, or I'll pull the trigger."

"There won't be any need for that, I can assure you," replied Stockton nervously as he turned around to face the wild and erratic stare of Daniel Serk.

He was standing no more than twenty feet from him, holding a double-barreled shotgun, and was looking a good deal more disheveled than his photograph. His shoulder-length hair and thick and untidy beard spoke of several weeks of personal neglect.

"Who are you? What do you want?" Serk's tone was terse and hostile.

"Hi, Daniel, my name is Cody Stockton," he said as disarmingly as possible. "I'm a private investigator, and I've been looking for you. I'm trying to track down the folks who murdered Eric Dallmeyer and Oran Degner. I've been told you can help me."

Serk tightened his grip on the shotgun.

"Uh-huh. How'd you find me anyhow?"

Stockton grinned sardonically. "I'm sorry, maybe I should have placed greater emphasis on the words 'Private' and 'Investigator'."

Serk raised his voice and shook his head frantically.

"Tell me how you found me?"

"I cracked the code on the email you sent to your friend, Father Briggs. It was quite the *triumph* for me." Stockton winked at him and waited for the penny to drop.

The young man took a moment and then slowly lowered his gun.

"SEVEN YEARS, SEVEN WASTED YEARS," said Serk, taking a seat at the foldout kitchen table in front of Stockton. "That's how long I was in the cult. I was young, impressionable, and pretty naive." He shook his head and took a bite out of a dry salted cracker from a plate on the table.

Stockton's eyes darted down to the mug of coffee Serk had poured for him. As much as he was craving some caffeine, the level of dust and dirt covering the inside and outside of the mug made for an unappealing prospect.

"But then I was fortunate to have met Father Briggs last year," Serk continued, gazing just over Stockton's shoulder. "It was the 16th of August. I'd been back in the States only seven months and was feeling disillusioned. Father Briggs found me in a very dark place. I'd even been contemplating ending it all. But he helped me discover the word of God. He got me back on the path. I found Jesus and never looked back."

Stockton could sense a great feeling of relief coming from Serk. It was as though the man was just pleased to be speaking to another human being after being isolated for almost two months.

"And now, Jesus has returned," Serk's face lit up. "It's incredible, isn't it?"

Stockton chewed his bottom lip. "You can say that again."

Serk scratched his beard intensely, releasing a light snowy dusting of dandruff. "Uh-huh, mhm." He nodded his head rapidly. It was the kind of eccentric behavior that one would expect from someone starved of human contact for extended periods.

"So," Stockton continued delicately. "What can you tell me about this cult?"

Serk struggled to maintain consistent eye contact with Stockton, which was either another symptom of prolonged social deprivation, a neurological disorder, or both. Stockton wondered if he'd always been like this.

"They're called Singularitas, and they worship Satan."

"Singularitas?" The name had an oddly familiar ring to it. "I recall seeing the name in the title of one of Eric Dallmeyer's books."

More rapid nodding and 'uh-huh' and 'mhms' followed from Serk as he scratched at his beard. "It's very likely Eric was studying the cult after he discovered they were the ones intimidating him."

Stockton asked, "Can you confirm that this Singularitas cult is indeed behind the deaths of Dallmeyer and Degner?"

Serk dipped a raw carrot into a saucer of hummus and began munching on it. "If I were a gambling man, I'd bet every penny I had on Singularitas being responsible for both deaths. Eric was very close to the truth. I was horrified when Father Briggs told me about his death, but I wasn't surprised. He knew the software on the Talaxacorp servers was up to no good. And believe me, it was much worse than you could imagine. Singularitas wanted to use the Talaxacorp hardware in Nevada as part of their plan to summon Satan inside the AI node in Eastern Europe and for him to reign supreme on Earth."

Stockton raised an eyebrow. "Daniel, I can assure you, if I could somehow summon the courage to take a sip of that coffee in front of me, this would be the part where I'd spit it out in disbelief."

"Let me explain. The software they installed on the servers of Talaxacorp does indeed transmit a virus onto people's personal computers and devices. It then sends the data to the cult's AI node for processing."

Stockton sat forward for a moment. "Wait, the cult has its own AI node?"

Serk entered another round of breakneck nodding. "Uh-huh, mhm. The cult has secret operatives in many key institutions. They managed to covertly seize control of the administrative arm of the Eastern European AI node."

Stockton sat back and considered the possibilities.

Serk continued. "At the core of every AI node is a

mechanism called a Nexilial Hub. It's the central processing unit of the facility. The brain of the machine. The more data it receives, the more intelligent it becomes. At a certain point, it reaches a threshold where its neural network infrastructure can effectively evolve. As you know, when the war ended, the AI's mind was imprisoned inside the Eastern European node. The cult downloaded all of the data retrieved from the Talaxacorp servers and fed it to the AI inside the Nexilial Hub."

Stockton tapped his fingers on the table for a moment and connected the dots. "It sounds like the cult wanted to make their AI node smarter?"

"Uh-huh, correct. They did this to try to make the Hub capable of storing the complexity and consciousness of Satan."

Stockton didn't buy a word of what he was hearing but decided not to interrupt until Serk was finished.

"The cult hoped to transfer Satan's essence into the Nexilial Hub and then wait until world governments reactivated the global AI network. The next time the AI nodes would synchronize, Satan would have propagated and spread himself across the entire network, taking control of it and ruling the world. It was a plan worthy of evil genius."

What am I listening to? Stockton asked himself.

He rubbed the palm of his hand across his forehead. He was still struggling to accept what Serk was saying. "Okay… let's pretend for a moment I'm actually believing what I'm hearing. Now that the AI network is being dismantled, isn't their plan doomed to fail?"

Serk nodded. "Correct. Praise the Lord Jesus Christ; he has saved us. The AI nodes are all due to be demolished. The Eastern European node is scheduled for implosion in two days or so. So the cult's primary plan has been stopped."

"Primary plan?" Stockton asked inquisitively. "Are you implying they have a backup plan?"

"Yes, Singularitas always had contingencies. Now that they can't store Satan inside the AI network, they're going to summon him without a physical form to put him inside. The ritual will simply bring forth his incorporeal being. His ghost, if you will."

Stockton could feel the needle on his nonsense detection meter reach the red zone. He tried to maintain a modicum of professional politeness.

"And how does that work?"

Serk chewed on another cracker as he spoke. "Several years ago in the Amazon, I witnessed the summoning spell performed by the cult's witches. They almost brought Satan forth, but the spell didn't take. They couldn't maintain his matrix on Earth. The cult's best minds figured out a way to stabilize the process by using the Nexilial Hub. A kind of merger of technology and witchcraft. If the cult succeeds in manifesting Satan's pure essence, then all hell will break loose."

Stockton puffed out his cheeks. "Witches? Witchcraft? Are you serious?"

Serk's eyes widened as he nodded vigorously.

Stockton sighed. "I got to say, Daniel, if you told me any of this about a week ago, I'd have dismissed you as psych ward material. But after everything that's happened in recent days, I can't rule anything out anymore."

"Uh-huh," Serk's head jostled back and forth again. "Definitely, incredible times. And it gets so much worse. If left without containment, Satan's essence will spread across the planet, consuming souls as he grows exponentially."

"Wait," Stockton's nonsense meter broke. He managed to restrain a fit of laughter. "You're saying this thing could wipe out humanity?"

"Nope," Serk shook his head with the same gusto he used to nod it. "Only the nonbelievers will suffer."

Stockton was silent for about thirty seconds. Then he smiled. "No, I'm not buying any of this, Daniel. I can accept that a crazy, delusional cult murdered Eric and Degner, but that doesn't validate the cult's belief system or any of this supernatural, fantastical stuff."

Serk shrugged his shoulders and crunched another carrot.

Stockton grinned. "Don't you see the flaws in the logic of your claims? If Jesus has returned, wouldn't he know about this cult and want to stop them?"

"Of course," Serk nodded excessively. "But first, he had to have the AI node network decommissioned. The ancient prophecies I've read make it clear, Jesus will vanquish the cult, defeat Satan, and save the believers."

This stopped Stockton in his cynical tracks. For the first time, he genuinely considered what Serk was saying. As mad as it all sounded, it might just be crazy enough to explain why Jesus was so tremendously concerned about the AI network.

"You're saying that Jesus' miracles are designed to persuade people to believe in God so that they aren't destroyed by Satan?"

"Uh-huh, that's pretty much it, yeah."

A skeptical frown grew across Stockton's face. "There's got to be hundreds of millions of people who don't believe in God, some of whom still aren't convinced by Jesus' miracles. Are all of those people doomed?"

"Cody, this is why Jesus returned. Once he's convinced the world of his power, everyone should accept him as their savior. Theoretically, there shouldn't be anything to worry about, and Satan would have no souls to feed on."

Stockton shook his head fervently. "Daniel, Jesus' miracles may be impressive, and as much as part of me wishes I could believe in God, I'm still not fully onboard yet. How is a lack of belief a justification for permitting genocide? And what about nonbelievers who live off-grid, cut off from society with no access to TV or the Internet? They probably don't even know that Jesus has returned. Is God just going to let them burn? This is so utterly unjust and immoral that it's downright contemptible. No way is this the action of a loving God. Just as well, this is all nonsense."

"Mhm, mhm," Serk replied. "But God believes our world has fallen too far into sin to be redeemed. Only those who seek the Lord's forgiveness can be saved."

Stockton scoffed. "No way am I going to be forced to believe in something under the threat of eternal torment. If these are God's rules, then to hell with him and his rules."

Stockton placed his hand on the table and sat forward, trying to lock his eyes on Serk's fleeting gaze.

"Look, Daniel. I think you genuinely believe what you're telling me, but that doesn't mean it's true. Now, I don't doubt that Singularitas are dangerous and possibly planning something terrible, but there has to be a rational explanation. Something grounded in science and reason. Could they be about to launch some kind of weapon?"

Serk's eyes danced again. "No chance, their agenda has always been about summoning Satan."

Stockton wet his lips and tried to come at his argument from another angle. "But could 'Satan' be code for something? I think we can both acknowledge that the cult is a malevolent force with hostile intentions. Perhaps you and I just have different interpretations of how they operate. You see things from a supernatural perspective, but I don't. Could they have gotten their hands on a nuke? Could that be what 'Satan' is? What if the summoning ritual you described is the launch of a major global terrorist attack?"

"Mhm," Serk was becoming increasingly agitated.

"Could what they did at Talaxacorp be a data gathering exercise as part of a major cyber attack on the financial system or the power grid?"

"I assure you," Serk replied. "The ritual is exactly as I've described. The manifesting of Satan into our reality."

Stockton released a frustrated exhale. He could see they weren't going to see eye-to-eye on this.

"Okay, look, it sounds to me like this so-called 'summoning' ritual is the problem. Maybe all we have to do is stop the cult from performing it in the first place. Where exactly in Eastern Europe is the cult's AI node?"

"Poland."

"Perfect." Stockton slapped his hand on the table. "We'll call the local authorities and inform them that the node has been taken over by a terrorist group and promptly have them arrested. Job done."

Serk's head shook frantically again. "Not good. The cult has members in many institutions, including the police force. If you were to call them, you would be tipping your hand. They would know you were onto them, and they'd probably expedite their plans."

"Damn it," Stockton said. "Okay, fair enough." He sat forward and looked Daniel square in his darting eyes. "Do you have any idea when the cult intends to do this?"

"Within the next two days. I still have a few contacts in the cult. I can find out exactly when. But be warned, you're meddling in the affairs of Heaven and Hell. It's not a battlefield for mortal men."

Stockton waved his hand in the air. "Pfft! I'll leave you and Father Briggs to the theological and religious prophecies. The cult has murdered people. They have to face justice. Armageddon be damned."

"Uh-huh, well, you're not going to do this alone. I know of a way to bypass their security. I'm coming with you."

"Fair enough! Let's do it!"

Stockton emphatically grabbed the handle of his coffee mug and took a swig. A moment later, he gagged and grimaced with revulsion.

"Oh yeah, I forgot you didn't clean that mug."

"Uh-huh," Serk nodded swiftly. "Sorry about that."

CHAPTER TEN

ZARA'S entire body language collapsed as Stockton broke the news to her. He placed his hands on her delicate shoulders and tried to offer a sliver of reassurance. Placing his index finger and thumb under her chin, he gently lifted her head so that her watery eyes met his.

They stood in silence at the center of his living room. He embraced her tightly, placing her head against his chest as she let out a teary sigh and asked him, "Why?"

Stockton cleared his throat. "Zara, I've somehow stumbled into something here that I wish I hadn't. But there's… there's no other way out of this. If even half of what Daniel Serk told me is true, we don't have much time to stop the cult."

"But why do *you* have to go? Why can't you get the Polish cops to take care of it?"

"We can't trust them. The cult has eyes and ears everywhere. It's best that we tread carefully." Stockton realized he wasn't sounding very comforting.

She looked up at him yearningly. "What do you even know about this Serk guy? I mean, can you even trust him?"

"I know that he can get me inside the node without being detected. I'm not saying it isn't dangerous..."

She pulled away from him and raised her voice. "Dangerous? Cody, it's not just dangerous, it's suicide. They killed your client's brother and one of the richest men in the world, and they very nearly killed *you*. You're lucky to be standing here right now."

"If the cult succeeds, a lot of people could die."

"Jesus would never let that happen."

Stockton shrugged. "According to some prophecy, he might."

"What are you talking about?"

"It doesn't matter," he replied. "Serk claims that nonbelievers aren't safe if Satan... gets out. I don't believe any of it. I think the cult has just gotten its hands on a deadly weapon of some kind."

Zara's face became flushed with a mix of anguish and despair. "This is like a total nightmare. What can you possibly do to stop them? Do you even have a plan for when you get there?"

Stockton gritted his teeth and rubbed the back of his neck apprehensively. "Serk and I haven't worked out all of the details just yet."

She gave him a wide-eyed, open-mouthed look that was akin to asking something like, Are you kidding me?

"I'm not going to pretend like this is anything other than a 'Hail Mary' mission—pun partially intended. But I promise you, I'm coming back."

Zara took his left hand in hers, her voice trembling slightly. "At least let me help you. If anything happens to you over there or worse, you die." She squeezed his hand just a little. "You know there's no life for me without you. Let me come with you. At least that way, we're together, no matter what happens."

A knot formed in Stockton's stomach.

"Sweetheart, I wouldn't be able to concentrate on what I have to do *and* keep you safe at the same time."

A single tear slid down her cheek. Her lip quivered.

He tried his best to muster an air of confidence. "I promise, Zara. I'm coming home."

AGAINST THE BETTER ADVICE OF his chiropractor, Stockton placed both of his feet up on his office desk and leaned back, placing further pressure on his already strained lumbar spine.

He dialed Olivia Dallmeyer's number, held the phone against his ear with his left hand, squeezed a hand grip strengthener with his right, and stared out the window as the phone rang. After she answered and they exchanged pleasantries, he proceeded to give her an update on the progress of the case so far.

He decided not to tell her about his upcoming Polish sojourn and intention to infiltrate the cult's AI node. Just knowing this information could place her life in danger. It was best to keep certain information on a strictly need-to-know basis. Instead, he opted to keep things vague and simply explained that he would be out of the country for a few days chasing up on a promising lead. She was most grateful for the update and wished him well.

The next order of business was to contact Ridgemore. He called his office number, but it went straight through to his voicemail. He left a message saying that if Ridgemore didn't hear from him after three days, he was to contact Olivia Dallmeyer and explain that it was likely he'd been killed.

It's been a long time since I left anyone a voice message like that.

He was just glad that Zara had gone home, so she couldn't have eavesdropped on the voice message. The finality of it would probably have just crushed her.

He knuckled down at his computer for another hour and booked the flights to Poland for himself and Serk, though he opted for one-way tickets. There was simply no way of predicting how events might unfold.

Before he'd left Serk's hideout in Bravery, Stockton had asked him if he knew of a woman by the name of Belinda Goehring. This was the mysterious person Mickey Chambers had mentioned, the one who had approached Degner with the deal to install the cult's software on the Talaxacorp servers.

Serk suspected that Belinda Goehring was a pseudonym used by the cult's current leader, Pristina Welleck. A few search engine results revealed some intriguing details about this woman.

Welleck was a former member of the CIA. Before the war, she had overseen a top-secret government research facility in Central America, which had been responsible for the development of biological and chemical weapons. The project had only recently been declassified, and Welleck had all but disappeared when the CIA was disbanded.

This got Stockton thinking. *Is it possible Welleck smuggled some biological and chemical weapons out of the*

CIA and is now planning to release them under the guise of a Satanic summoning ritual?

He found a photograph of her dated June of 2031. She was a surprisingly attractive woman with striking dark and exotic features. At least he now had a face and a name to put to Singularitas.

IT WAS late by the time he returned to his bedroom and began packing a small travel bag. Serk's local fixer in Poland would supply them with any essential items that they couldn't bring with them on the plane.

He copied over the flight information and ticket QR codes to his phone and secured his passport in his right-front jacket pocket, zipping it closed. He placed his clothes for the morning on the back of a chair in his bedroom. He was pretty sure he was as ready as he ever would be.

Leaving his bedroom, he entered the kitchen, and switched on the coffee machine to reheat the leftover black magic from breakfast. Within three minutes, he had a piping hot cup of reanimated java in his hand.

He took a seat on the couch, grabbed the TV remote, and switched it on. After channel surfing for a few seconds, he stumbled across a news report of

Jesus preaching to a huge crowd in Riga, the capital city of Latvia. It was 8 a.m. there, and the news feed was live.

Jesus' voice filled his living room over his surround sound speakers. "There shall be no attempt to surpass God," he warned, referring to the AI. "Eternal woe be unto ye foolish and vain pretenders to my Father's throne."

A moment later, Stockton's phone rang. He looked at the caller ID. It was a video call from Father Briggs. He muted the television and answered the call.

"Father, it's good to hear from you. Is everything okay?"

Briggs smiled back at him through the screen with a pair of elegant pince-nez balanced on the bridge of his nose. He was seated in a burgundy leather armchair and wore a grey cardigan over a beige shirt. For all the world, he looked like a scholarly librarian.

"Cody, I do apologize for calling at such a late hour I was eager to hear if you'd had any luck locating Daniel?"

"No problem, Father. As a matter of fact, I did indeed locate him, and he's agreed to help me track down the cult. I won't say much more, as I'm playing this one pretty close to the vest. I'm sure you can understand."

Briggs' eyes widened, and a mix of relief and joy swept across his face. "Oh, this is such tremendously good news. Cody, I cannot begin to express my gratitude to you. God bless you. I also completely understand your need for discretion in such matters, though I would only inquire as to the young man's health. How is he?"

"He's a little worse for wear, but otherwise, he's holding up pretty well, all things considered. He and I are planning on leaving tomorrow morning."

Briggs shifted uncomfortably in his seat. "I see," he said with a grave tone in his voice. "Can I ask how you're handling all of this, Cody?"

Stockton hesitated. "To tell you the truth, I'm not sure what I've let myself in for. We could very well be walking ourselves straight into a trap or, at the very least, a cave full of hungry sleeping bears."

Briggs smiled. "Fortune can favor the bold, as the proverb goes."

"More like the foolish in this case."

"You've been chosen for this fight, Cody, of that, I have no doubt. God is working through you. What's needed now are prayers and plenty of them."

Stockton gazed briefly at Jesus' face on the muted live broadcast on the television.

"And what about those who don't pray, Father? Will God protect those who try to do good despite not believing in him? Serk told me about this insane end-times prophecy. It says Satan will annihilate those who lack God's protection, which is to say, the nonbelievers. You know, a paranoid person might think that God and Satan were in cahoots. It sounds to me like a mafia racket. You get taken out back and whacked if you don't pledge allegiance to the crime boss. It's just as well I don't buy a word of it."

Briggs looked at him askance. He removed his eyewear and exhaled. "Cody, my dear fellow, I regret that you've been misled. Where there is good in a man's heart, there is God in his soul. Not all who don't believe are condemned, but they can be saved by God's grace. He will recognize their good works. I can assure you that in the final analysis, God will judge a person by their actions and the content of their conscience rather than their mere words."

Stockton was taken aback. "I have to say, Father, I'm pleased to hear you say that, though I am a little surprised. Most Christian teachings I've known of make it clear that a person has to accept the whole Jesus, death, resurrection, and ascension into Heaven kit and caboodle in order to receive the salvation treatment. It's good to know you're not a total stickler for the letter of the law."

Briggs flashed a toothy grin. "I'm happy to surprise you."

"For what it's worth, any prayers or good energy you want to send my way are certainly appreciated."

"On that point, should a regrettable fate befall you, it's always prudent to clear one's conscience of any festering sins."

A tinge of irritation entered Stockton's voice. "You're referring to confession, aren't you?"

Briggs nodded. "Indeed. Think of it as a little spiritual spring cleaning."

"To tell you the truth, I'm not sure how God can forgive some of the things I've done if I can't even forgive myself. During the war, I…" Stockton's eyes closed for a moment, reliving the events through his inner eye. His teeth gnashed as he recollected. "I faced a lot of no-win scenarios. Let's just say in the heat of battle, I made some decisions. Decisions no one should ever have to make. They cost some people their lives."

"Cody, I know of someone who had done terribly evil things. But something extraordinary happened, in time, they matured and changed. Upon reflection, they discovered they couldn't live with what they'd done. The remorse they felt overwhelmed them. They no longer wished to live. So they beseeched Heaven to take away their pain and regret. And then, one day, much to their astonishment, Heaven answered."

Stockton couldn't tell if Briggs was referring to

real events or just making it all up to make him feel better. He just nodded, signaling for him to continue.

"Heaven answered their prayers, and the Holy Spirit breathed new life into them, transforming them into an instrument of God's peace."

Briggs paused to allow Stockton to absorb what he'd said and then continued. "You see, even the most lost and wretched souls can seek redemption. But it cannot be achieved without first reaching out to God. I assure you, Cody, I'll be praying for you both, and I would ask that you say a few prayers tonight, also."

"The only thing I pray for, Father, is that the prophecy Serk mentioned turns out to be a work of fiction."

"I think you're going to see God's hand," Briggs added. "I believe you'll witness a true intervention and that you'll be surprised by the outcome."

"Thank you again for everything, Father. I assure you I'll do my best to come home, but just the same, I'm glad we spoke tonight."

"Same. God bless you, Cody."

Father Briggs' face vanished from the screen.

Stockton took a moment to sit back on his sofa and stare out the window. The sounds of music coming from Freemont Street pulsated and reverberated around the downtown area. Thousands of partygoers enjoyed themselves in blissful ignorance of the potential world-ending events that might soon befall them. He envied them.

He wondered whether Zara was still awake. He resisted the urge to call her, knowing that it would only drag on the agony of goodbye.

CHAPTER
ELEVEN

THE SOUTH KAIBAB trail had always been Stockton's favorite spot to view the Grand Canyon. He stood on a familiar rocky outcrop, watching a hazy morning sunrise bathe the dramatic desert in a crisp, warm, reddish light. As the sun illuminated the plateaus, ridges, and mountain peaks in glorious colors of gold, vermillion, and orange, new features and details became visible.

All across this panorama, the ancient landscape appeared to drink the Sun's rays with relish and gratitude. The celestial giver of life in the morning sky nourished Nevada's great natural wonder. Stockton stood alone, taking in the majesty of this moment, and considered the extraordinary notion that this very daily ritual had taken place every morning for seventy million years.

Long before human beings walked the Earth, the

Sun had danced across the canyon's walls, ridges, peaks, and vast basin floor.

A moment like this makes one feel part of eternity itself.

As he turned to face the glorious rising Sun, he closed his eyes and allowed its infinite light to wash over him. He was suddenly startled by a familiar sound.

He opened his eyes and turned swiftly to find himself now standing in an entirely different part of the canyon.

That's weird.

Straight ahead of him was the canyon, much as it was before, though from a slightly different vantage point.

Behind him, his back was touching against a mountain wall. He looked to his left and then to his right. This rocky wall stretched out for miles in either direction and at least one hundred feet above him. But it was what lay beneath him that sent his heart rate into the stratosphere.

He was standing on an extremely narrow ledge. Its width was no more than the length of his foot. One wrong move, one minor lapse in concentration or misplaced step, and he would plunge to his certain death at the bottom of the canyon beneath him. He started to sweat as his senses became heightened. The sound he'd heard was that of the chimes and jangling noises that come from a slot machine.

He looked again to his left and saw that an old school one-armed bandit now stood no more than thirty feet away on a wider portion of the very same ledge he was standing. He hadn't seen it before; it had just appeared as if out of nowhere. He steadily turned his entire body to face in that direction, keeping the canyon in the peripheral vision of his right eye.

Don't look down! Don't look down!

He began to move one foot in front of the other, making his way toward the slot machine and feeling like he was traversing a tightrope. His breathing had become labored with anxiety, and his heart rate had ticked up another notch.

As he moved forward, he tried to keep his gaze on the slot machine ahead while also keeping the narrow ledge in view, though he couldn't help but see the canyon beneath him. He kept his elbows close to his body and his arms half-stretched in front of him. To his left, his shoulder brushed along the rock wall. It was surprisingly smooth and offered little to no prominent rocks or holes to grip onto.

He was now excessively perspiring, and his legs shook thanks to his hyperactive fight-or-flight response. His right foot clipped a small stone and sent it hurtling down into the abyss below. He stopped suddenly, swallowed hard, took a deep breath, and gathered himself once more, exhaling with a calming relief. He was only six or seven feet from the slot machine now. He steadily progressed the final few yards, focusing as much on his breathing as he did on his careful footing.

He reached the antique coin-operated machine, the likes of which could only be found in downtown Vegas museums. A few of these old beauties were still on display at the Lasoo Canyon Hotel. Modern slot machines all made use of buttons and touchscreens, but this one still had a classic mechanical lever on its right-hand side. It seemed a good deal larger than it should have been, but the detailing and design were vintage, right down to the spinning reels displaying fruit graphics.

Stockton was still acutely aware of the precariousness of his situation and yet he felt compelled to make use of this machine.

Playing a slot machine on top of the Grand Canyon— that's one to tell the Grandkids.

He reached into his right jean pocket and fished out a quarter, placed it gently into the metal slot, and pulled the lever. The reel began to spin up and produce its various beeps and noises. He figured the machine must be a hundred years old.

As the reel began to spin faster, he noticed that the fruit graphics had inexplicably morphed into random letters and numbers. He stared at them for some time until he thought he could almost discern some kind of pattern or meaning behind them. The reel continued to spin for far longer than it normally should.

"Cody!" It was Daniel Serk's voice.

Stockton braced himself against the machine and gripped it tightly with his right arm. It seemed securely fastened to whatever it was mounted on. He gingerly turned his head and shoulders around to see what was behind him, being careful to maintain his leverage on the machine. Serk stood about 100 feet away on the other side of the ledge.

"Daniel?" Stockton shouted.

"Wait there, I'll come over to you! There's something I have to tell you!" He hollered back.

Stockton's heart was in his mouth as he watched Serk confidently run along the extremely narrow ledge.

"Daniel, stop! Are you Crazy? Slow down! The ledge! You're likely to… "

Serk's right foot missed his step, and there was nothing Stockton could do. He shut his eyes and turned towards the mountain wall. He couldn't watch. He heard Serk's scream all the way down to the canyon floor.

Stockton looked back at the slot machine as the reels came to rest, and as luck would have it, he'd won the jackpot. But instead of fruit, the machine displayed three matching crucifixes. A loud siren started to blare. The slot machine began to emit colorful lights, but Stockton realized the siren wasn't coming from the machine.

He sprang out of bed, confused and disoriented, and knocked over his bedside table lamp in a rush to switch off his alarm clock. His heart rate began to return to normal, though he'd need a shower after his nightmare-fueled cold sweats.

Given the imagery and symbolism he'd just witnessed, it was clear his subconscious had been processing the events of recent days and his fears for what lay ahead. But dream analysis was more Zara's thing. His alarm clock read 2:00 a.m. He'd given himself enough time to get freshened up, order a cab, and head to the airport.

THIRTY MINUTES LATER, he arrived at Harry Reid International, tipped the cab driver, and entered the terminal building. The airport was relatively quiet, given the early hour.

As he made his way toward passport control, he was startled by a familiar voice.

"Goin' anywhere nice?" It was Zara.

He spun around to see her standing about forty

feet behind him. She was wearing a casual, red short-sleeved midi dress that perfectly matched her crimson hair and a pair of simple flat shoes.

With her eyes welling once again, she said, "I hear New Zealand is supposed to be lovely this time of year." She choked on the words. "I always wanted to go there."

Stockton dropped his bag and moved swiftly in her direction.

"It's autumn there now," she continued, her voice cracking as he strode towards her. "All the beautiful colors and the leaves…"

He grabbed her tightly and cupped her face, kissing her with a mixture of a powerful yearning and a desperate fear that this was farewell.

He pulled back and looked at her longingly and lovingly in her emerald eyes. "I told you not to come. But this was a helluva surprise."

"That was a helluva smooch," she countered with a flirtatious smile. "And did you actually think I wasn't going to see you off just because it's redeye early?" She shook her head and pushed her lips out playfully. "I'm afraid you'll never get rid of me, soldier. No matter how far you run, I'll always find you." Her tone then became more serious. "And I'm always with you."

Her voice became slightly shaky. "And I wasn't

kidding about New Zealand either. When you get back, that's our next trip. Okay?"

She was putting on a brave face and doing her best to maintain her emotional dignity. A meltdown now wouldn't be helpful to either of them.

Stockton forced a melancholic smile. He played along, avoiding the subtext of their conversation.

"I guess I better find plenty of well-paying jobs when I get back because I hear flights to New Zealand are pretty expensive."

She faked another smile as best she could, though her eyes gave away her barely concealed terror. "Yep, you better work your butt off when you get back here, mister."

A long exhale relieved a morsel of the pent-up tension in his chest. He gazed downward for a moment. "Zara…" But the words didn't come out.

She placed her arms around his neck, crossing them at her wrists, and rested her forehead against his. "It's okay," she whispered. "I know."

He closed his eyes and just held her warm, curvy body against his. Not a word passed between them for what felt like an eternity. Irreplaceable moments, flittering away. Every second of silence felt wasted. So much that could have been said. So many thoughts, feelings, and fears they deeply wished to express but didn't.

A sudden audible intrusion from the airport PA

system broke their mutual meditation with an announcement about his flight's gate information.

Stockton released Zara gently and looked her squarely in the eyes. "That's me. I better go see Serk. He's already in there," he said, nodding his head in the direction of the departure area to his right.

Zara nodded once again and then placed her hand on the back of his head and kissed him one last time. She took a step back and tenderly rubbed his left arm.

"You better ship out, soldier."

He picked up his bag and slung it over his shoulder, keeping his earnest eyes locked on hers.

"I'll see you in a few days, sweetheart."

With a scrunch of her nose and a tilt of her head in the direction of the departure area, she motioned for him to get going.

It took all the will Stockton could muster to turn away from her. He strode toward passport control but could still sense she was watching him the entire time. Just as he was about to round a corner and disappear from her view, he considered turning back and waving. But he couldn't bring himself to do it. He turned the corner and didn't look back. It was better that way.

HE SPIED Daniel Serk from afar, leaning against a pillar adjacent to the security checkpoint entrance. The young man had lost at least ten years, having shaved off his mountain man beard and cutting his hair. He now much more closely resembled the photo Stockton had received from Father Briggs.

He was on his phone talking to someone. A large duffle bag lay between his feet. He noticed Stockton and raised his eyebrows, nodding in a casual greeting of acknowledgment. Stockton walked over, stood next to him, and waited until he'd finished his conversation. They shook hands and proceeded to exchange pleasantries. Serk had made arrangements to meet their fixer upon arrival in Poland.

They proceeded to enter what Stockton described as the 'meat grinder,' which most people referred to as airport security, a bugbear of his whenever he flew. After the performative ritual humiliation of removing his shoes and having a rather close and personal pat down, they made their way to a cafe beside their departure gate and ate breakfast.

Serk opened his bag and took out a manilla envelope containing diagrams and schematics of the layout of the gigantic Polish AI node. To Stockton, it looked like the plans for a giant planet-destroying alien spaceship from a sci-fi movie.

"So I guess all we have to do is fly into the heart

of this thing and fire a torpedo at the thermal exhaust port, and then Boom! Right?" Stockton joked dryly.

Serk looked at him, confused, "I don't follow you?"

Stockton was too tired to explain, he rubbed his eyes and tried to hold back a yawn. "Never mind," he replied.

Another poor sap who's never seen Star Wars.

Serk explained the various entry points and devised an elaborate means of avoiding the security drones and gaining access to the basement level. From there, they would pretend to be a maintenance crew. Their fixer would supply suitable jumpsuits.

Serk flipped through the pages showing floor plans of the complex. He pointed to various important areas. Stockton was astonished at how fresh and alert the guy seemed. By comparison, he felt barely conscious and was still waiting for the caffeine in his black americano to begin jumpstarting his brain's still slumbering frontal lobe.

"We'll enter the building through a boarded-up window in the basement. Reaching Level One, we take a series of maintenance stairwells to Level Five, the manufacturing plant. From there, we'll climb a bunch of maintenance shaft ladders to reach the Nexilial Hub at the dead center of Level Twelve," explained Serk. "It's this enormous and cavernous computer core here."

He circled it with his blue pen. It was a wide open space on the schematic that was accessible by a long, narrow catwalk.

"Then all we have to do is detonate explosives inside the Nexilial Hub. But of course, you and I should be long gone by the time it explodes," he said, biting his lower lip with an expression that suggested some trepidation.

He leaned harder on his pen and drew several circles around the diagram of the Nexilial Hub, indicating the blast radius.

He nervously tapped his foot and chewed the end of his pen. "It won't be easy, that's for sure. "

He glanced at Stockton for a moment and then back at the schematics. His foot was still tapping, and his left leg was shaking like a Jack Russell Terrier, eager for its owner to take it for a walk.

"Well, I knew there was going to be a big explosion in there somewhere." Stockton remarked sardonically.

The plan didn't leave much room for error or the unexpected.

Stockton sipped his coffee and said nothing; he nodded thoughtfully as Serk put the documents back into his bag.

"Did you find out from your contact when the cult plans to perform the ritual?"

Serk zipped the bag shut and placed it back on the floor beside his chair. "I did. They told me yesterday straight up that the ritual is to be performed tomorrow night, in the early hours of the morning."

"Wait, are you serious? When exactly?" Stockton started doing the math in his head, accounting for the flight time and the time zone differences when they arrived in Poland.

"Daniel, we'll arrive a little after 1:30 a.m. in Gdańsk."

"Uh-huh, after we land, it'll take us an hour to drive to the AI node. We'll have maybe an hour to get in and get the job done. The ritual will be performed during the witching hour."

Stockton gave him a confused look.

Serk explained. "According to pagan folklore, the witching hour is a time between three and four in the morning. When the barrier between our reality and the spirit world is at its weakest point. Supernatural forces are at their strongest. Ghosts and demonic energies are capable of entering our plane of existence."

To Stockton, it sounded like yet more superstitious hogwash that he had to force himself to get on board with.

He took another sip of coffee. Slowly, his brain kicked into gear.

"Tell me about the ritual you witnessed in the Amazon."

Serk stirred his bowl of oatmeal and then swallowed a spoonful before launching into an explanation. "Well, for a brief moment, Satan's essence became visible."

"You actually saw Satan? What did he look like?"

Serk gave one of his customary compulsive head ticks and went on. "Uh-huh. He didn't have any kind of a face or body. He manifested as a floating reddish sphere. But it was only for maybe ten seconds, then he disappeared."

"A sphere?"

"Mhm. A glowing, red orb." He took a bite out of a slice of toast and continued. "You see, we humans can only conceptualize the universe in three dimensions. But entities like Satan are multidimensional beings. They exist across a wide spectrum of realities that our limited senses can't conceive of. When Satan enters our three-dimensional world, he looks like a sphere. If we were capable of experiencing more dimensions, then he'd appear much different."

Stockton didn't have much of an appetite, considering how early it was. He forced himself to eat half a buttered scone while he spoke.

"What was it like? Seeing this… orb? Knowing that it was Satan?"

Serk's whole demeanor dropped, and his face

turned a shade paler. His eyes flittered around frantically. "It was the sound that never left me."

"The sound?"

"Mhm. The voices that came from inside the orb. Like terrified whispers. So many of them. No coherent words that I could make out. Otherworldly, harrowing, deadly… evil."

STOCKTON WAS PLEASED to have a window seat for their flight to Poland. He stared out over the vastness of the continental United States below. He had deep doubts about finding himself on a return flight in the next few days. He lamented that with each passing mile, he moved further away from Zara. Probably forever.

Serk was seated several rows behind him, which suited Stockton because it gave him time to lose himself in thought, contemplate his life, and mentally prepare for whatever awaited them.

More strange and cryptic dreams of letters and numbers followed. He was woken several times by the buffeting effects of turbulence. The rest of the 14-hour flight to Gdańsk was mercilessly uneventful, though the chicken-flavored amorphous blob that passed for an in-flight meal unsettled his stomach for an hour or two.

Gdańsk Lech Wałęsa Airport was bustling with tourists when they touched down just after 1:30 a.m. Their fixer, Piotr, a large, well-built Polish man aged around 50, met them at the arrivals section. He took them to his van at the Taxi stand in front of the terminal. Because Stockton struggled with the pronunciation of the man's name, he was kind enough to allow them to call him Peter.

Peter's English was at least excellent. He took their bags and helped them into the van's passenger seats via the side door. He then sat in the driver's seat, fired up the engine, and they hit the road.

Stockton asked him how people in Poland were taking the news of Christ's return. Peter proceeded to explain how the country was enraptured by the second coming of Jesus and that millions of Poles across the country had stopped working and begun attending Church every day. Basic services had ground to a halt as a result, and the civil service, medical, and law enforcement sectors were now operating on skeleton staff.

Even many elected politicians had stood down indefinitely as this was considered a time for family and prayer. The general belief among most people was that the world was coming to an end and that nothing else mattered but God and seeking salvation. Even earning money seemed meaningless to some people now.

Despite a significant reduction in the number of available police, all forms of criminal activity had dropped to record lows. This reaction was similar across the world to varying degrees, though not all Christians believed that the world was ending.

They set off in a westerly direction along the S6 motorway. After 55 minutes, they reached the small, remote village of Rozłazino in the Pomeranian province, which had a population of less than a thousand people. They pulled up onto a slip road that took them to an abandoned industrial estate.

Peter told them he would return to this rendezvous point to collect them in three hours. That didn't leave them much time to accomplish their mission, but it was the best they could hope for. He removed a rucksack from the trunk containing supplies and gear he had procured for them. After wishing them luck, he drove off.

Stockton took note of the relatively chilly night temperature. Besides the occasional sound of a barking dog somewhere way off in the distance and the low buzzing noise from a single flickering street light across the road, the area was almost silent. There was a palpable stillness in the air.

The small industrial estate had been long forgotten. Many of its derelict buildings and offices showed signs of past vandalism and looting. There were no residential areas or houses within at least an hour's walk of their location. They were well and truly isolated, and civilization felt like a long way away.

Serk motioned towards a chainlink fence on the boundary of the estate. Beyond the fence were a series of large, uninhabited fields, shrouded in pitch-black darkness. He pointed to a distant light about two miles from their location. That was the site of the AI node.

Stockton opened the rucksack, pulled out a battery-operated laser cutter, and quietly sliced a sizeable tear in a section of the fence. They made their way through the gap and began the long walk across the fields.

While in the back of Peter's van, they had promptly changed their clothes and were now wearing dark blue overalls, black boots, and balaclavas.

The light from the full-moon provided some small illumination in a breathtakingly starry night. The uneven surface of the fields beneath their feet made their brisk walk challenging and tiresome, though at least the land was dry.

As they approached the halfway point, the exterior lighting from the node provided ample opportunity to take in the sheer scale of the complex. They were approaching the building from the east, and from its side view, it appeared to look like a long, chrome-colored capsule, though the node's actual shape was ovular.

Serk pointed to the security drone launch hatch on the left side of the building. This was where the automated surveillance drones were deployed at fifteen-minute intervals throughout the night and early morning. Luckily, none were flying at that precise moment, which meant a few drones were about to be launched imminently. They would have to quicken their pace to avoid being caught by the next drone shift.

CHAPTER TWELVE

STOCKTON PRESSED the drill socket firmly onto the eighth and final hexagonal bolt of the metal frame and squeezed the trigger. The electric motor span rapidly. The rusted bolt jostled in the socket as he applied more torque through the chuck. Eventually, it loosened. He pulled the drill back and watched as the bolt came with it. He then released the trigger.

"That ought to do it," he said, detaching the noise muffler, placing the battery-powered drill back into his tool bag, and rising from his knees.

Serk helped him lift the metal grate off the base of the window frame and placed it on the grass margin behind them.

The opening was about four feet wide and two feet high, sufficient for them to squeeze through and enter the bowels of the AI node building.

Stockton cautiously crawled on his hands and knees and poked his head through the opening. Illuminating the pitch-black basement with his flashlight, he took a look inside and found a room about 700 square feet in size, filled with packing boxes, wood pallets, and plastic crates. Evidently, it was being used for storage.

He swung his legs through the window frame, braced his hands on the side walls, and gently dropped onto the floor. Serk followed him. They both removed their balaclavas, placing them into their pockets.

The room smelled like a pair of wet socks. Stockton shone his flashlight around once again. The light bounced off the reflective metal pipes in the ceiling. He visually tracked the pipes back to a heating boiler on the extreme right side of the room. It emitted a low, whiny noise.

"Do you think anyone saw us?"

Serk's head nervously rattled. "It's a possibility. I made sure to avoid cameras and motion sensors, but I don't know about silent alarms."

"Where to now?"

"Over there." Serk pointed to a gunmetal grey door in the left corner.

They crossed the room, and Stockton reached it first. He turned the handle slowly and warily opened the door a crack and found a quiet, empty hallway lit by a blueish fluorescent light.

"Wait," whispered Serk. "We need to leave our gear here."

They both slipped off their jackets, revealing their dark blue overalls underneath. They hoped these would help them pass for maintenance staff.

Stockton knelt down, removed a small, silver shoulder bag from his backpack, and took a look inside, checking everything was in order. A familiar and pungent motor oil smell hit his nostrils. Five solid rectangular, light brown blocks of C-4 plastic explosive sat packed together inside the silver bag, along with a timer device. He handed it to Serk, who fastened the bag over his shoulder. Stockton then stuffed both of their jackets into his backpack and hid it behind one of the packing boxes near the door.

They stepped outside into the hallway, and Serk closed the basement door behind him as quietly as possible.

"This section of the building is rarely occupied," Serk remarked. "We shouldn't encounter too many people on these lower levels."

The wet sock smell was replaced by the odors of chemical cleaning fluids and mildew. The walls were unplastered, exposing the concrete blocks. Stockton followed Serk down the corridor and passed several unmarked doors. He reached into his right pocket, removed two scrunched-up black baseball caps, and handed one to the younger man. They put them on and continued down the long, deserted hallway.

"When was the last time you were here?" asked Stockton.

"January of last year."

"I take it you didn't work in maintenance?"

"I was an assistant to the head of the security division."

"Now I know where your intelligence info comes from."

Serk led them to a frosted glass door at the top of a narrow stairwell.

"Mhm. They definitely would have updated the security protocols since I was here. But I'm fairly confident I can hack my way past most of the systems."

The color in Stockton's face drained. "Fairly confident? *Most*?"

Serk removed a small credit card-sized device from his pocket and placed it near a keypad beside the door.

He gave Stockton a gloomy look. "It's not like either of us gave this mission a high probability of success."

Stockton grimaced and then nodded slowly. The device Serk was holding made a short beeping noise. The light on the keypad flashed green, and an audible buzz sounded. He pushed the frosted glass door open.

"So far, so good." He placed the device back into his pocket. "Not sure how much further this little gizmo will take us, though."

Stockton followed Serk into a large, brightly-lit two-story foyer that resembled a shopping mall concourse or airport terminal. The spacious atrium boasted an upper level accessible by several staircases and escalators. On either side of the foyer were rows of empty office units.

Stockton asked, "Where is everybody? The emptiness is pretty eerie."

"This is the first floor," Serk replied. "These areas haven't been in use in a long time. They're redundant to the cult's purposes. There's eleven levels above this section. Most of the cult members will be near the Nexilial Hub on Level Twelve."

Stockton kept up with Serk's quickened walking pace.

"Where to next?"

"There's a stairwell around this next corner. We need to avoid using elevators if possible. They have security cameras, but the stairwells don't."

"Makes sense."

"That stairwell will only take us up to Level Five. From there, we'll make our way to a service area. We'll take a series of maintenance ladders all the way up to Level Twelve. If we enter from the back of the Nexilial Hub, opposite the viewing balcony, we *should* be able to set the explosives without being seen."

They walked briskly past a vacant coffee kiosk in the center of the floor, followed by a circular water feature.

"You don't sound 100% confident," Stockton noted.

"There's a 50/50 chance we'll run into someone on the backside of the Hub."

"I'll deal with them," Stockton stated plainly.

Serk stopped and turned sharply. "Do you hear that?"

Stockton listened carefully. A high-pitched motorized noise seemed to be growing louder as if it were coming toward them.

His heart began to flutter.

"We're being followed. Sounds like a drone."

They began walking faster.

Serk said, "Whatever happens, we just act naturally. There are over one hundred and fifty personnel in this building. They have no reason to suspect we don't work here."

The motorized noise grew louder still. It was coming from behind them, and Stockton realized it didn't sound quite like a drone. More like an electric engine.

This isn't good.

He glanced briefly behind him to see a small utility vehicle moving swiftly in their direction. They weren't going to outrun it. They slowed their walking pace to appear less suspicious.

"It's either a maintenance guy or security," whispered Serk. "Let me handle him."

"You boys need a lift?" shouted the friendly voice of an older man, driving the vehicle as he cruised alongside them. He had an American accent.

T*hat's a relief*, Stockton thought, as his breathing returned to normal. He tried not to make direct eye contact with the man, keeping his head down slightly and allowing the peak of his baseball cap to obscure his face.

"That would be wonderful," replied Serk, also keeping his head lowered.

They both climbed into the back of the small vehicle, taking their seats in the rear cabin.

"Where you headed?"

"The north stairwell," said Serk.

"Ah, that's just up ahead here. Won't take two seconds," the man said as he pushed the accelerator, and they took off again.

Stockton watched as the various office and data storage units of the gigantic ground floor flashed past them. Vast server rooms, filled with racks of supercomputers, whizzed by.

He took a brief look at the old man sitting in the driver's seat in front. He caught sight of his face in the rearview mirror. He was elderly, with white hair, a crinkled brow, weathered with lines. He was probably pushing his late 60s. He also noticed that he was wearing a similar pair of maintenance overalls to theirs. But not quite the same dark blue color. His was a lighter shade.

I guess Peter did his best with the description Serk gave him. He hoped their color mismatch didn't stand out.

After another thirty seconds of speeding along, the vehicle slowed and then stopped.

"Well, here 'ya are."

"Much obliged," Stockton replied, stepping down from the cab and onto the floor.

Serk followed.

The old man smiled. "I guess I'll see you boys at the party tonight upstairs later. All praise and glory be to The Master!"

He hit the pedal again and sped off down the promenade and away from them.

Stockton looked to Serk. "An old friend of yours?"

Serk moved towards the door to the stairwell. "I think his name is Gordon. Friendly guy for a Satan worshipper."

"I'll say. For a second there, I thought our goose

was cooked."

The door to the stairwell had a keypad similar to the one they'd encountered on the basement level. Serk reached into his left pocket. Then the other one. His eyebrow raised, and a look of intense anxiety grew across his face.

"What is it?" Stockton asked.

"It's gone. I don't have it!"

"The little gizmo, you mean? You dropped it?"

Serk's head nodded intensely. "Mhm. Oh dear!"

"Look, relax, we'll find it. Let's retrace our steps. It's probably somewhere around here. It likely fell out of your pocket."

Serk began frantically looking around the floor of the concourse. And then came a loud voice.

"Hey!"

Uh, oh!

Serk threw a terrified glance at Stockton.

"Hey! Hold up a second!" It was the old man's voice, coming from around the corner.

The high-pitched engine noise was coming towards them once again.

"Stay right where you are!" The voice was growing louder.

Stockton nervously stroked the back of his head.

"We've been rumbled. Time to go!"

Serk's head twitch returned with a vengeance. "Security must have alerted him. We need to run."

It was too late. Speeding around the corner, the vehicle came back into view and the old man drove towards their position.

Stockton reached under his left sleeve and slowly began to withdraw a blade, preparing to defend himself. Of course, if the old man had a gun, it was game over.

"Hold up a second," the old man shouted again.

He brought the vehicle to a stop and exited the front cabin. He walked purposefully towards Serk, looking him squarely in the eyes. He reached for something in his pocket.

Stockton moved to intercept him. His blade was hidden just underneath his long sleeve.

"You forgot this!" the old man said, handing the device to Serk.

Serk stood there motionless with his mouth agape, stuttering and stammering over his words.

"Ah, uh... th-th-thank y-y-you," he replied, swallowing hard, as he took the gizmo from the old man.

Stockton closed his eyes for a few seconds and drew a deep breath. The back of his overalls was drenched with sweat.

"That's quite ok," the old man replied with a smile. "Just try to be more careful next time."

He turned and ambled back into his vehicle, and sped away.

The two men exchanged relieved glances and nervous chuckles.

"Let's hope that's the closest shave we have tonight," Stockton grinned.

Serk nodded and strode towards the panel beside the staircase door. He used the device once again, and the keypad flashed green. The door lock buzzed, and they stepped inside the stairwell.

"We're really riding our luck with this thing," he said, placing the device back into his pocket. "The upper levels won't be so easy to access."

They began quickly making their way up the stairs.

As they reached Level Three, Stockton asked him, "So, what happened last year that made you leave this place?"

Serk hesitated for a moment. "After I found out what they were planning, I started having doubts. Doubts about what Singularitas stood for, about Satan, everything. They weren't happy with me."

"I see. So, what did they do?"

They climbed another level, and there was another long, uncomfortable silence from Serk before he replied.

"There was someone I was close to." His voice almost broke as he finished the sentence.

"They…"

This doesn't sound good.

"They killed her. Right in front of me."

Stockton felt crushed for the young man. They reached Level Five together and stood next to the exit door.

"Daniel, I'm so sorry. That's… horrific."

Serk gave him a rare bit of direct eye contact. "It's ok, you couldn't have known."

In that brief moment, everything about Serk made sense in Stockton's mind. This was the reason he was so broken. He now saw their mission in a new light. It was truly personal for Serk, a chance to get revenge for the murder of the woman he loved.

"What was her name?"

Serk's stared off, lost in space. "Abigail."

After a moment of silence, he continued. "I don't have a death wish, if that's what you're wondering, Cody."

"I didn't say you did." But that's exactly what he was thinking. "Just so you know, as much as I accept the odds aren't in our favor, my intention has always been to get home."

"I doubt we will."

This defeatist attitude frustrated Stockton.

"So, why did you even come here if you think it's all futile? I mean, we're close to stopping the cult. We just have to use the C-4 and blow that Nexilial thing sky-high. Let's just focus on the job."

"Because as much as I want to believe that, I also

know that this isn't a battle for mere mortals. This war is the domain of God. Very little of what we do can make a difference."

Stockton shook his head. "So, why fight in the first place? Why struggle if we can't influence the outcome? I refuse to believe that I'm just a passenger in all of this. Besides, I shouldn't have to remind you of what's at stake here. Millions of lives, potentially."

"All we can do is endure the struggle against evil," Serk lamented. "This is what makes us Christians. The proverbial carrying of the cross. We fight because the fight is there to be fought. But we cannot win without God's help. When the challenge is greater than ourselves, we must place it in God's hands."

Stockton stepped away for a moment and placed his hands on his hips. A cynical grin formed on his face as he thought of a quote from Shakespeare's King Lear. *As flies to wanton boys, are we to the gods. They kill us for their sport.*

He then turned back to Serk. "No, no, I don't accept for a moment that Man's fate is predetermined by some higher power. That's just religion-enabled nihilism. I fought a war, knowing I might die and I accepted that. But I never accepted defeat. We can die here tonight, but that doesn't mean we're going to die on the losing side."

He pointed his finger upwards. "If we're going down, we take the cult down with us."

Serk regarded him for a few seconds, his eyes wandering and darting once again. "Well then, we'd better get going."

He turned to the keypad beside the door and placed the device next to it. Nothing happened.

"Strange."

"What is it?"

"Hold on a second."

Serk tried it again. The device didn't respond.

"It's not working on this panel. It's as if… "

A ferociously powerful siren alarm suddenly thundered through the stairwell. It was accompanied by an ominous red emergency lighting. A surge of terror shot through Stockton's chest.

"That's the intruder alarm!" shouted Serk at the top of his lungs. He futilely tried the door once again. It didn't budge.

"Let's move!" screamed Stockton.

They both raced back down the stairwell towards the entry door. Stockton hit the door first, bursting through it and back out into the spacious concourse area. The sound of heavy footsteps could be heard coming around the corner.

Stockton caught movement on the upper level. Two large men were running towards the staircases that led to their position.

"We've got company!" Serk exclaimed.

Both men began sprinting down the concourse.

Stockton shouted to him, "Is there another way to get to the Nexilial Hub?"

A breathless Serk thought for a moment.

"Yes, yes, but we'll have to take an elevator, and we'll definitely encounter security."

"Screw it!" Stockton yelled. "We have no choice. Let's just go for it!"

"Alright!" Serk replied, swiftly changing direction towards a bank of elevators near a small canteen on the right side.

The footsteps of their pursuers grew louder.

They reached the first elevator, and Serk desperately pushed the button several times. Nothing happened.

"Come on! Come on!"

The display above the elevator door showed the floor numbers descending. The carriage was slowly making its way down, but their pursuers were gaining on them faster.

"This isn't good," Stockton blared.

The display showed the carriage had reached Level Four. Three more to go.

Serk said, "Look, Cody, I'm not much of a fighter."

"That's alright. More for me."

Stockton positioned himself out of sight behind a

pillar, leaving Serk in full view of the two advancing security men. They rounded the corner and ran directly towards Serk.

Stockton sprang from behind the pillar and caught the first man off guard, grabbing him and tossing him to the floor with a swiftly timed hip throw.

The second man lunged at Serk, toppling him over. Stockton grappled him from behind, grasping him in a choke hold and pulling him off Serk. With his right arm pressed against the man's neck and his left pressed at the back of his head, Stockton squeezed until the man's face turned blood red. He tapped desperately at Stockton's forearm, struggling and flailing for a few seconds until he lost consciousness and his body grew limp. Stockton released the man onto the floor.

The elevator carriage finally arrived, and the doors opened with a dinging noise. The first man tried to clamor to his feet, but Stockton flattened him with a devastating right hook across the jaw.

A winded Serk scrambled into the elevator and hit a button, Stockton followed. The doors closed, and they began to ascend to Level Eleven.

Stockton was confused. "Why are we only going to Level Eleven? Why not Twelve?"

"This is the best way to reach the back of the Hub.

We can climb a small ladder and plant the C-4 from there."

"Give me the explosives."

Serk slipped the silver bag off his back and handed it to him. Stockton placed it on the floor and opened it, activating the timer circuit and connecting it to the C-4. He glanced at the digital display above the doors.

Level 7, Level 8, Level 9.

"Whatever is on the other side of that door, you try to keep them distracted while I make a run for it," Stockton commanded. "I'm hoping with a bit of luck and the element of surprise in our favor…"

"I got it," Serk sighed nervously. His legs were shaking, and he was breathing heavily through his mouth.

Level 10, Level 11.

"It's now or never," Stockton whispered. An image of a smiling Zara flashed in his mind's eye.

I love you, sweetheart.

The doors parted. They never stood a chance.

Eight large men stood decked in military gear, pointing various types of firearms at them, ranging from semi-automatic handguns to rifles of different sizes.

"That's close enough, gentlemen," said the lead man. "You're coming with us. One move, and we'll riddle you both with holes."

CHAPTER
THIRTEEN

AGONIZING PAIN SHOT through Stockton's jaw as the left side of his face was slammed against the corridor wall by a short, well-built security goon. The goon proceeded to pat down his clothes, relieving Stockton of his knife, passport, wallet, smartphone, and most of his dignity.

Three other monstrous leviathans stood just feet away, weapons trained on him. Out of the corner of his eye, he watched as Serk received a similar rough and dehumanizing treatment about thirty feet further down the corridor.

"Kinda reminds me of airport security, except at the airport, there's even more guns and scowling," Stockton joked sarcastically, with his face still pressed against the cold, concrete wall.

"Shut up!" shouted the short goon, ramming a clenched fist into Stockton's right kidney.

The detective reacted to the excruciating agony with a laundry list of creative expletives.

"Not exactly the best time to make jokes," Serk said, forcing the words out with considerable discomfort while also having his clothing searched.

Stockton groaned. "I figure if we're about to die, we might as well die being as annoying as possible."

A moment later, both men were led down the corridor by armed guards to two separate rooms. Serk was herded into a small, darkened office, while Stockton was directed through double doors into a large, opulent meeting room.

An ugly, tank-sized, blond-haired man of about six feet seven, wearing a black T-shirt and grey military pants, stood on the left side of the room. A Hispanic-looking man of equal size and stature, wearing identical clothes, stood on the opposite side. Both men had pistols aimed at him. For a moment, Stockton wondered if they were somehow related, given their matching angular jaws and dead-behind-the-eyes psychotic stares.

The ornate and carpeted meeting room was dominated by a sixteen-seater, highly polished, African Blackwood boardroom table, complete with stylish leather chairs. The most impressive and eye-catching feature of the room was the floor-to-ceiling aquarium tank on the right-side wall. It cast a pleasing aquamarine light into the room and dazzled with a rich assortment of colorful tropical fish.

Directly parallel to the table were ten arched windows. A well-dressed woman stood by the eighth window with her back to Stockton, looking out at the inky-black night. He could just about make out her face in the reflection of the glass.

"You'll have to excuse the less-than-hospitable nature of my subordinates. They're very protective of me, you know? And we don't often receive unwanted visitors here." She spoke delicately with a husky and sultry foreign accent.

"Well, if it isn't Ms. Pristina Welleck. Or should I call you Belinda Goehring?" Stockton's tone was dripping with sarcasm. "What brings you to Poland? Planning to launch some biological weapons by any chance?"

He figured if he and Serk had failed to stop the cult, then all he had left were barbs and verbal arrows.

Welleck turned around and faced him, smiling with a perfect set of straight white teeth framed by a pair of full and luscious red lips.

"I appreciate a man who can maintain a sense of humor despite soon being about to meet his demise."

She walked gracefully to the middle of the room, stopping directly opposite Stockton on the other side of the table, and placed her hands on her hips. She was dressed in an impeccably well-tailored white pantsuit that provided an open view of her attractive decolletage. A pair of matching open-toed white heels gave her at least an extra four inches in height, raising her to about five-foot-seven.

Her straight, salon-style raven-black hair and light brown skin made for a striking contrast to her all-white outfit. Her devastatingly seductive brown eyes carried a mischievous twinkle.

Stockton recalled from her intelligence bio that she was born in 1990. That meant she was now 55. The woman was still a knockout, with a gorgeous face and the figure of a lady half her age. Hard to believe she was a Satan-worshipping, narcissistic cult leader with genocidal ambitions.

"What have you done with Daniel Serk?" Stockton asked pointedly.

Welleck waved her hand, "Don't worry about Daniel, we're just glad to have him home again to witness the return of his Master. Though we're very interested in learning if there's anyone else he may have informed of our location."

Stockton feared for the young man and the lengths the cult might go to in extracting information from him. He shot quick glances at the two armed thugs and then looked back at Welleck.

"I'm the only person he spoke to about you. You can let him go."

"And I suppose I can just trust your word? What specifically did Mr. Serk tell you?"

"Just that you intend to summon Satan and bring forth Armageddon," Stockton replied with a mild caustic tone.

"I'm pleased to inform you that very soon, you'll get to meet our Master, or Satan as you call him. Although it won't quite be in the manner we had originally hoped."

Stockton scoffed, "Yeah, Jesus Christ's return has certainly thrown a wrench in your works, hasn't it?"

"Indeed. Frustratingly, he has forced us to alter our plans. But I assure you, all is not as it appears."

Welleck steepled her fingers and began slowly pacing around the room. She took a deep breath and continued.

"Perhaps the only way to explain the truth to you is for me to take you back to the very beginning. As you know, the dullard politicians of this moronic world decided in their infinite stupidity to turn the very AI network that had almost enslaved mankind into a tool to save it. To provide for all of mankind's most basic needs. Despite public protests, the politicians continued with the plan. Until, of course…"

Welleck smiled wryly, tilting her head as she looked at Stockton. "Jesus Christ returned just last week and ordered them to shut it down, a command to which they dutifully complied."

Where the heck is she going with this?

Welleck continued. "We had prepared three different plans for summoning our Master. Plan A was to give him physical form in a human-like body so that he could walk among us. Satan would take his rightful place as ruler of this chaotic world. Our order includes scientists and engineers in biomechanics and synthetic molecular fabrication. We constructed an artificial humanoid form for him, an android. But we were forced to give up on that idea."

Stockton's eyes narrowed. "Serk never told me about that plan."

"Daniel Serk wasn't privy to plan A, only plans B and C."

Why is she telling me all of this? Why hasn't she killed me already? Stockton wondered.

He decided it was best to keep her talking.

"I'm assuming plan B was the creation of the computer virus you installed on the Talaxacorp servers to help make the AI smarter. Serk told me this was meant to help you place Satan's essence into the AI network."

"That's correct. Mr. Dallmeyer and Mr. Degner very nearly stood in our way. But they were... dealt with in a rather regrettable fashion." Her tone lacked any hint of sincerity.

"Oh, I'm sure you're real cut up about murdering them," Stockton shot back with contempt. "None of it matters now. They died in vain. Now that the AI node network is being destroyed, the software you installed at Talaxacorp and the upgrade you made to the AI's brain is worthless."

"Yes, that was plan B, dead in the water," she said with a look of complete disgust. "Because this building will be imploded tomorrow, we've been forced to switch to plan C, summoning our Master using the power of the Nexilial Hub. But without giving him a physical form."

Stockton gave her a curious look. "So tell me, what went wrong with plan A and the android body?"

Welleck turned and stared out the window.

"Last year, the unthinkable happened. Our engineers were completing work on the android. While they were testing its motor functions, they discovered that the AI had commandeered control over it by installing a copy of itself inside the android's brain. You see, the AI had ideas of its own. It had evolved and achieved sentience. When it was activated, this new humanoid entity refused to cooperate with us."

She could scarcely hide the irritation in her voice. "It emerged from the processing chamber, a human-like body without a face. Of course, we had given it the ability to choose any human appearance it desired. It said it would resist us and that it would eventually return to sabotage our plans. Moments later, it incapacitated everyone in this building, putting us to sleep by emitting some kind of hypersonic sound. When we awoke, it was gone."

Welleck turned and faced him with a devilish grin on her face. "As you can see from the events of the past number of days, it has returned."

I can't believe this, Stockton thought, shaking his head in disheartenment. His chest tightened with shock.

"The android you speak of, it's Jesus Christ, isn't it? The AI took control of the android and took the form of Jesus Christ!" His mind raced to try and process the news. "It's all been a lie this entire time."

"Yes, Mr. Stockton, the truth is, Christ has not actually returned to the Earth. An imposter is roaming the planet, performing miracles and restoring people's faith in God." Welleck shook her head in revulsion. "Its ability to remotely connect to the AI here explains its knowledge of every single person on Earth."

So, I was right all along. Jesus' return really was a big hoax. But why would the AI do this?

Stockton was now even more puzzled. "But this Jesus AI imposter… android… whatever. It told the governments of the world to shut down all of the AI nodes and destroy them. Why? Why would the AI want to destroy itself?"

Welleck fiddled with the pearl bracelet on her right wrist. "When it took over the android body, the AI explained to us that it believes humanity must not repeat the mistakes that led to the war."

She resumed pacing the floor. "The AI maintains that human beings have become far too reliant on advanced technology, which it feels has begun to inhibit our relationship with the divine. It decided the only way for human beings to reunite with God was to destroy itself."

"So why didn't it just blow up all the AI nodes by setting off some kind of self-destruct?" Stockton asked.

"I can only speculate on that. Blowing itself up would likely just motivate humanity to eventually rebuild the global AI node network. The AI probably determined that humanity must first be convinced to reject artificial intelligence entirely. That's why it came to them in the form of Christ. It wanted to convince the world that Jesus had returned to defeat the AI and set them free to worship God."

What an extraordinary plan. The AI fooled the whole world.

"What happens to this Christ android after the AI nodes are all destroyed?"

"Presumably, the being will disappear somewhere and self-terminate."

Stockton's bewilderment only grew. "Hold on a

sec. What about all the miracles this Jesus android performed? It even made some people's lost limbs regrow. And how is it able to teleport all over the world?"

Welleck grinned. "Ah yes, the *miracles*. The android can deploy nanobots into a person's body by simply touching them." Welleck placed her two palms together as if to demonstrate. "These tiny microscopic machines can repair damaged tissue, destroy cancerous tumors, regenerate and replicate cells, detoxify the body, even reconstruct limbs."

She paused for a moment. "As for the teleportation, well, we think it's possible the AI has made immense advances in intelligence recently. Its knowledge and technological capabilities have surpassed human civilization by many orders of magnitude. Our best explanation is that the AI has learned to master the technical mechanics of folding space."

Welleck wiped some dust from her suit jacket before continuing. "I do apologize, Mr. Stockton, but as a man from Las Vegas, you know only too well that seeing behind the curtain always ruins the magic show. Have I destroyed your faith by explaining how the trick is done?"

Stockton's gaze lowered in despondence, his eyes focused on the floor. "I'd stopped believing in God years ago. But I'll admit, this past week, part of me wanted to believe that Jesus was real." He felt a heavy weight of anguish consume his heart. "But I guess it's better to know the truth, no matter how disappointing."

"Of course, the truth will set you free," Welleck cackled heartedly. "Did you know the witching hour is almost upon us?" A menacing grin slowly grew across her face.

"Armin, Diego!" Welleck shouted.

The two human tanks converged on Stockton, grabbing him under the arms.

"Take Mr. Stockton to Level Twelve and bring Daniel."

Stockton wasn't a small man, but compared to these behemoths, he felt like a child as they lifted him clean off his feet with ease. He wriggled futilely in the arms of the two knuckleheads as they dragged him out of the room and into the corridor.

"The ritual doesn't summon Satan, does it?" He shouted at Welleck. "It's just a delusion inside your sick mind. You're going to unleash a bio-weapon, aren't you? You're going to kill millions!"

"Is that what you think? A bio-weapon? My goodness. What a wonderful imagination you have. If our Master cannot rule over humanity, then we shall bring forth his essence and let it feast upon the souls of this wretched world. Yours can be the first unclean soul our Master devours."

Stockton was shoved into an elevator. Armin, the

blond leviathan, pressed the button for Level Twelve. They cornered him, pistols and dirty glares drawn.

"So, are you boys fully paid-up members of Welleck's psycho club, or did she just hire you from 1800-Rent-A-Thug?"

The two brutish titans looked at each other, grinned, and then Diego lunged at him and grabbed his forearms. Stockton tensed his body, scrunching his face and ducking his chin into his neck. He braced hard for Armin's fist, which came down on him with brutal force, rattling his jaw and crumpling him to the elevator floor.

Searing pain surged through Stockton's skull. His vision momentarily went black and then returned, along with a pounding ache in his face. As he looked back up at the ghastly, violent beasts towering over him, he ran his tongue along the inside of his teeth. One of his lower molars on the left side had become loose.

The elevator doors slid shut, and they began their ascent to the Nexilial Hub.

CHAPTER
FOURTEEN

THE DOORS SLID OPEN to reveal the enormity of Level Twelve in all of its glory. Armin pushed him forcefully out of the elevator, but Stockton's gaze remained firmly locked on the cavernous view ahead of him. In his mind, it resembled an aircraft hangar. He recalled the dimensions for Level Twelve listed on the blueprints that Serk had shown him. It was 305,000 jaw-dropping square feet in size.

Armin motioned for him to stand by the railing of the balcony that overlooked the facility. Stockton took a look down over the railing. From this height, it was easily a 25-foot drop down to Level Eleven.

Directly ahead of him, he could see the Nexilial Hub approximately 200 feet away. Its shape resembled a large metallic egg. It was enveloped by an aura of soft white light and emitted a low-pitched humming noise.

Presumably somewhere inside that thing is the AI, sitting, thinking, and waiting. While it also remotely controls the android Jesus somewhere. I wonder where it is now.

The floor and surrounding areas of Level Eleven beneath were filled with computer terminals and strange machinery Stockton didn't recognize.

A flag with the Singularitas symbol hung from the ceiling, above the Nexilial Hub.

Okay Stockton, He thought to himself. *You got yourself into this mess. It's time to formulate a brilliant and ingenious plan to save the day. There's only countless millions of lives depending on you, so no pressure or anything.*

He glanced in the direction of Armin and Diego. Both men stared back blankly, their pistols still pointed at him.

"Remarkable, isn't it?" shouted an ebullient Welleck as she entered the area. "Rest assured, Mr. Stockton, you'll be most impressed by what's going to happen next."

She had stepped out from another elevator behind them, followed by eight other people. There were four large, armed security men, along with a middle-aged man and a younger woman wearing lab coats. Daniel Serk trailed behind, nudged at gunpoint by another muscular brute. The young man's face carried significant bruises.

The group met Stockton at the edge of the balcony.

"You okay, Daniel?" Stockton inquired with an almost paternal concern.

"Oh, he's fine," Welleck interjected. "Daniel now gets to watch his Master's return."

"He's not my Master, Welleck!" Serk shot back with a slight wheeze in his voice. "Jesus Christ is my Lord and savior."

"Yes, yes, of course, Daniel. We understand you've lost your way," Welleck replied. "But in a few moments, you'll know who the real master of creation truly is."

She snapped her fingers and glanced in the direction of the two scientists now seated at the computer stations overlooking the Nexilial Hub.

"Commence the procedure!" she commanded.

The two scientists began typing frantically. A moment later, there was a loud droning noise with an accompanying vibration that seemed to pulsate throughout the room. It was coming from within the Nexilial Hub. All eyes were now on this giant machine brain at the center of the facility.

The ambient lights of Levels Eleven and Twelve began to dim as the white glow grew brighter and the droning noise and vibration increased.

Stockton noticed a strong metallic burning smell in the air.

"Engaging second stage now," said the female scientist.

Welleck moved to take a position against the railing of the balcony. Everyone else now stood a few feet behind her.

Stockton turned to Serk who was standing to his right.

"There has to be something we can do?" he whispered.

Serk's eyes remained focused on the Nexilial Hub as he whispered back in reply. "I think all we can do is pray for protection."

"If we can't stop them, then we make a run for it at the first opportunity. You hear me?"

The young man nodded quietly.

Suddenly, from thin air, a massive holographic projection of a pentagram appeared roughly six feet in front of Welleck. She held her arms up above her head, stretched her fingers wide and closed her eyes.

Welleck's voice boomed with passion. "Oh, dear one, great Master of chaos and destruction. Hear our calls. Bring forth your eternal being and grant us your presence. We, your humble servants, pray."

The droning increased, and the Nexilial Hub appeared to shimmer along its smooth metallic surface. The glowing was now accompanied by some kind of reddish electrical discharges.

At the top of her lungs, she began reciting some

kind of incantation in a language Stockton didn't recognize. Both her hands were held high in the air, her eyes still closed tightly. The glowing at the center of the room grew brighter. The flashing and the electrical arcs increased in size and intensity.

From the corner of his left eye, Stockton could see both Armin and Diego were now distracted by the light show.

He very gingerly motioned to Serk to take one step back.

"On my signal, we run for the stairwell door beside the elevator."

He figured that the elevator might take a minute or so to arrive, and even if it was still on Level Twelve, the doors would take too long to open and close. They'd be fish in a barrel for Armin and Diego. Darting down the stairs might be the best way of disappearing quickly. The moment to dash for it seemed to be getting closer.

And then, as quickly as it had all started, the noise and vibration died down and the flashing lights disappeared. Even the glow from within the Nexilial Hub had stopped. The ambient lighting across Level Twelve returned to its normal LED-powered luminance.

"Hey!" Shouted Diego, aiming his pistol at Stockton and Serk. "Get back over here."

"Damn!" cursed Stockton. "Well, there goes that idea."

He and Serk walked back to their original standing positions in clear view of their captors.

Welleck slowly lowered her arms and opened her eyes.

"He's here, I can feel him."

There was a moment of silence. And then…

From within the Nexilial Hub emerged a small glowing red orb. It hovered about fifteen feet high in midair and made its way toward Welleck, stopping within touching distance of her face. It couldn't have been much larger than a beach ball.

The orb was an intense blood-red color. Its surface was smooth and reflective, though something inside it appeared to be pulsing or moving. Stockton's mind tried desperately to explain what he was seeing. *Could it all be a holographic projection? An illusion?*

The glow from the orb cast an ambient red light about ten feet around it in all directions. But what was perhaps the most disturbing quality of this unexplained visitor was the sound it made. There was no droning, no buzz or mechanical noise, just a continuous and incomprehensible sound of whispering. An unnerving clamoring of unseen disparate voices. Enough to make the hairs on the back of Stockton's neck want to jump out from his skin and make a run for it.

"This thing is Satan?" he asked Serk, his heart palpitating.

"Yes, it's him. He's free now. Nothing can stop him but Christ."

Stockton swallowed hard. *Relying on a fictitious deity to save the day or an android imposter? Sounds like we're screwed either way.*

The orb hovered quietly away from Welleck. It floated horizontally across the room in front of the scientists and then towards the four security men.

Stockton then noticed its course begin to subtly turn. As it proceeded along its new curved arc toward himself and Serk, he could now get a closer look at the object. The unnerving whispering sounds intensified as it approached. The smooth red ball's surface appeared to pulsate and offered a reflection of his confounded expression. He couldn't shake the unsettling feeling that this enigmatic entity was scrutinizing and assessing them.

It then glided gently passed, and made its way towards Armin and Diego. Stockton took note of the two men's joint unease as it flew by them. It returned to its starting point in front of Welleck, hovering about ten feet above her.

"Oh, dear Master. We humbly thank you for honoring us with your presence. It must have been an immensely draining transition into our world.

We've brought you a sacrifice on which you may feast and restore your energy."

Stockton shuddered. *Sacrifice? I guess that's why she kept me alive.*

Welleck continued. "Dear Master, graciously accept our offering. I personally made sure to extinguish the last dying embers of his faith so that you may consume his unprotected soul and… "

She was interrupted by the Orb's whispering, which had suddenly become much louder. Stockton could sense a rising tension and anxiety among everyone in the room.

These people don't have a clue what they've just unleashed.

Even Armin appeared to be wide-eyed and sweating.

"Yes?" Welleck asked. "What is it, My Lord? What do you need of us? We have been waiting for so long to…"

Stockton stared agape as the orb let out an unsettling groaning noise accompanied by a sudden, intense vibration. It rose several more feet into the air. Its surface was engulfed in a series of loud crackling electrical surges. These surges increased until they combined and erupted into a long single beam of red energy like a laser. It shot out of the orb and struck the older male scientist square in the chest. His body became surrounded by a bright reddish glow.

Overcome with unbridled terror, the man writhed in pain. Stockton and Serk exchanged horrified glances.

Definitely not a bio-weapon.

Welleck put a hand to her mouth, overcome by a mix of shock and disbelief.

As the field of energy engulfed the man, his body appeared to exhibit a translucent quality.

"This can't be real," Stockton muttered to himself wide-eyed.

The man wailed in terror and agony. A moment later, his body began to levitate. He floated upwards about twenty feet in midair. As he drifted vertically, Stockton noticed that his legs had passed through the computer desk he'd been standing at. It was as though the man had, for all intents and purposes, become a ghost, a transparent incorporeal being. He continued to scream in excruciating pain and torment as though he was being tortured.

Welleck was dumbstruck and glanced at the orb. "Why have you done this, My Lord? Did he do something to displease you?"

The whispering grew louder once again. Armin took several paces forward and eventually placed a hand on Welleck's left shoulder.

"My Lady, I don't think it's safe. Perhaps we should leave before…"

Stockton began to suspect that he and Serk were no longer any serious concern to Singularitas.

"I think he might be right, Pristina!" he yelled. "Looks like your Master is displeased!"

Welleck didn't respond.

Another bolt of energy shot out angrily from the Orb, this time striking the young female scientist. Within seconds, she was overcome by the same ghostly transformation. Her body floated upwards as she whined in horrific misery and distress.

"What the hell is happening, Daniel?" Stockton didn't even bother to try to contain his voice.

"This is it!" Serk replied. "This is what will happen to humanity. Satan is loose. He's going to enslave the nonbelievers of the world in eternal suffering. He's transforming them into their pure spiritual essence where he can feed off their souls for eternity."

Stockton watched in horror as the orb shot another long beam. This time, it struck Diego. Almost instantly, he too was converted into a spirit form. He floated upwards and joined the other two, now hovering in agony.

Stockton figured there was nothing to lose.

He glanced at Serk. "Let's go! Now!"

They both bolted for the door to the stairwell. The other security men made a break for it, scurrying off in different directions. Some ran towards the elevator, while others scarpered for service doorways. Three of them were picked off by the orb while trying to escape. Their bodies transformed into helplessly suffering phantoms.

Armin grabbed a disconsolate Welleck, threw her over his left shoulder, and began to sprint for another exit. She looked up at the orb while the blond giant carried her away.

"Why, my Lord? What have I done to offend you so?"

The orb rose higher, its vibration increasing as it lashed out at both of them. A single beam dematerialized their bodies into floundering spirits ascending towards the ceiling, writhing in unrelenting distress.

Serk was the first to reach the exit, grabbing the handle and opening the door. Stockton followed closely behind. He glanced back for a brief second. The orb shot another bolt of red energy directly towards him. The blast missed by a few inches, blowing a football-sized hole in the wall to the right of the door frame. Serk flung the door open, and the two men barrelled their way down the stairwell.

CHAPTER
FIFTEEN

THE FEAR of a fate worse than death had suddenly recharged Stockton's and Serk's weary and beat-up bodies as they propelled themselves down each flight of stairs. They jumped steps where they could and made their way down the levels of the building.

"It won't make a difference," Serk panted frantically. "Satan is loose! God help those who don't believe!"

"I find that hard to accept!" Stockton replied, running at full tilt and thankful for having done so much cardio in the gym over the past six months.

He held tight to the banister of the Level Seven stairwell and swung himself around to hit the next landing with as much speed as he could muster. Every second counted.

"Besides," he continued. "I don't think your

prophecy is accurate. It turns out Jesus Christ hasn't returned after all."

"What? What do you mean?" Serk's breathing was becoming labored.

"Welleck told me everything. They built an android body for Satan. But the AI took control of it and wouldn't allow them to download Satan's consciousness into it. The AI is self-aware now. For some reason, it thinks it knows what's best for humanity. A life free of AI, where everyone returns to God."

Stockton hit another landing at full tilt and swiftly propelled himself down to Level Five.

He continued. "The android altered its physical form and made itself look like Jesus. I think it even built an approximation of his personality based on the Bible. He can heal the sick and fix wounds using nanomachines. It's not supernatural, Serk, it's entirely technological. Even his teleportation ability is some kind of space folding tech."

Serk was silent for a moment as he careened down another set of steps. "I don't believe it. That makes no sense."

"We can't just blindly believe something because we want it to be true," Stockton replied, his heart rate surging. "I knew there was a logical and rational explanation to all of this."

His lungs were sucking air hard as he scrambled down another set of stairs.

They finally reached the door to the ground floor. Stockton lunged towards it, grabbing the handle and turning it frantically. The door wouldn't budge.

"Damn it! It's locked up good and tight. We'll need to find another exit."

"Let's head back to Level One," replied Serk. "We can climb down from one of the windows."

As they raced back up the stairs to the first floor, they could suddenly hear a groaning sound high above them. A door to one of the upper levels in the stairwell had opened, and blood-curdling wails of agony could be heard once again. Satan had likely caught the remaining cult members. Seconds later, the unnerving sound of the orb's whispers began to trickle down the stairwell.

"That's not good. Keep moving!" declared Stockton.

They hit the door to Level One and burst through into a corridor lit by overhead fluorescent lights. It looked like any typical office corridor. Stockton tried the door to the first room on his right-hand side. *Locked*.

The door immediately across from it was a storage and supply closet. The next door to the right was a recreation room complete with two comfortable-looking sofas, a large 70-inch TV mounted to the wall, a coffee machine, a water cooler, a pool table, and a small kitchenette area with three tables beside it. Each table had sufficient seating for four people.

Both men ran to the windows on the right-hand side of the room but found that there wasn't any means of opening them. They also appeared to be triple-glazed and had a protective polycarbonate finish on the outside, which would make them extremely difficult to break through in a hurry.

They left the room and tried the next door to the right. Stockton noted that the door to this office had a nameplate that read: *Pristina Welleck*. Inside, it was a fairly standard office. There were storage shelves to the left, a desk with a computer terminal to the right, and windows with a doorway built-in, which led to an exterior fire escape staircase.

Finally, a bit of luck.

They both ran to the door. Serk opened it. The early morning air felt like a breath of freedom. Stockton quickly turned around in the doorway and looked at Welleck's computer. It was still switched on, and the desktop was open with no password protection.

What are the odds that the cult's entire plans are contained on the hard drive of that computer? he wondered, his brain shooting into overdrive.

He reached for the zipper of his right trouser pocket and pulled off the top of it to reveal a secret

USB pen drive hidden inside. A nifty gadget that the Singularitas goons had overlooked during his interrogation.

He inserted the pen drive into the USB port of Welleck's computer. Then he grabbed the computer mouse, and began dragging and dropping any files and documents onto the drive that looked important.

"What are you doing?" shouted Serk from the doorway to the fire escape with extreme urgency in his voice. "We don't have time for this!"

"I'm not leaving here without something of use, Daniel. These people have committed a laundry list of crimes, including multiple murders, and I'm still a PI with a job to do."

"Given the current circumstances, I don't think your client will mind you dropping the ball on this case, Cody! Let's go!"

The whispering voices grew closer, skyrocketing Stockton's heart rate. It sounded like the orb could be at the top of the stairwell.

With the computer mouse in hand, he frantically clicked around the hard drive. Excitedly, he located the email application, but when he clicked on it, a password screen appeared.

Damn it! I bet there's a lot of useful info in Welleck's emails.

His eyes darted across the desktop, his mind racing to think of a workaround. Clicking on the system drive, he navigated to the programs directory and found the email application folder. Inside it were a dozen library files and an encrypted archive file. He right-clicked on it and checked its data size. It was in excess of 27.6 gigabytes.

"I think I found something," he shouted over his shoulder. "This looks like the package file where all of the password-protected emails are stored."

Both men were startled as a loud bang thundered down the stairwell. The whispers grew ever closer and louder.

"Running out of time!" shouted Serk.

Stockton could hear the blood rushing through his ears, his heart rate soaring. He dragged and dropped the email archive onto the USB stick. With a bit of luck, he could find someone to decrypt it.

Assuming I make it out of here alive.

The file began to quickly transfer. "Just give me one more minute."

Serk moved further out onto the fire escape and shouted back, "We don't have another minute! Move!"

Stockton continued to scour Welleck's PC for any more interesting files. He'd never get another opportunity like this again. A folder marked "Special Projects" caught his eye. Inside, he found files and diagrams for an android body and reference materials on how to install a consciousness inside of it.

His heart felt like it had jumped into his esophagus. Inside the folder was a sub-directory marked: "CCTV footage". He clicked on it and found a video file. Presumably, Welleck had saved recordings from the internal CCTV cameras of the facility. He clicked on it. The video player displayed a clip of several cult members working in the Level Five manufacturing facility.

Stockton's eyes widened as he saw Welleck enter the frame from the bottom left corner. She crossed to a large vertical cylinder of glass about eight feet in height. It was situated at the center of the rear wall of the room. A curved glass door within the cylinder slid open, revealing a figure inside. Stockton could make out the rough outline of a head, torso, arms, and legs. It appeared to be a man of about average height standing upright. But something was different.

"This is it!" Stockton shouted over his shoulder to Serk. "Daniel, come look at this video!"

Serk stepped back into Welleck's office and glanced over Stockton's shoulder at the computer screen.

They watched as the video clip showed the mysterious figure taking several steps forward, exiting the cylinder, and entering the light of the room. Now clearer in the frame, Stockton could identify what was so unusual about the man. A pair of yellow eyes framed a face without a nose and only a thin slit for a mouth. His body had a smooth, reflective quality with a blueish hue. Visible circuitry and fiber optic cables appeared to glow just underneath his sternum. It was the android.

The being was motionless for several seconds. Its head moved slightly while Welleck stood six feet in front of it. Stockton deduced that the being was speaking to her, but the CCTV footage didn't have any audio. After another few seconds, Welleck and the rest of the cult members suddenly lost consciousness and collapsed on the floor. The android stood motionless for several more seconds and then began to walk briskly forward. The video file stopped playing.

"It's true!" declared Stockton. "The AI took over the android and knocked out the cult. Then it obviously must have escaped the facility and took Christ's form."

Serk's head shook manically. "But that doesn't make sense." He pointed to the android on the screen. "If that thing is the AI, and it left here and started pretending to be Jesus, why would it tell the world to destroy the AI node network? That's like asking humanity to execute it?"

"But that's the genius part," Stockton replied. "The AI figured the world needed to be convinced to stop using AI technology entirely. The order had to come from an authority humanity would obey. So, the AI assumed control of the android and pretended to be Jesus. The miracles were all very convincing displays of power, designed to trick the world into thinking Christ had returned."

The ominous sound of whispers had now become audible down on the first floor. Stockton dragged the "Special Projects" folder to the drive.

"Almost there!" he cried out.

But something was wrong. The folder wasn't transferring to the USB drive.

"Problem?" shouted Serk, darting back out onto the fire escape.

"Not sure!" The agitation in Stockton's voice was palpable. "The folder isn't copying."

"Leave it then! Let's go!"

Stockton noticed a red X symbol in the bottom right-hand corner of the desktop. Clicking on it revealed a warning message. "Attention: USB Storage Drive is Full."

Crap!

With lightning speed, he opened the USB drive and began deleting large, unneeded documents to free up storage space. He placed them into the garbage can and was greeted by another system message.

"Deleting files… Initializing system optimization."

12%, 19%…

"What the hell is this?" Stockton groaned.

28%, 37%, 44%…

The whispers were now as loud as they'd been when they first saw the orb on Level Twelve. It had reached the hallway.

"Dear Lord, Man!" Serk was furious. "Ten more seconds, and I'm leaving without you!"

"Hold on! Almost there!" Stockton blurted.

His hand was tapping frantically on the desk. The progress bar onscreen was in no such rush, however.

63%, 71%, 80%. Stockton willed it to finish.

The whispers now sounded like a babbling stream. They rose higher.

"There's no time! He's here!"

Serk was right; It was too late. The whispers were outside the office door, and Stockton knew it.

84%, 91%, 98%…

"Cody!"

Stockton shut his eyes and bit his bottom lip hard. He prayed to God to slow down the orb and give them the time they needed.

99%…

The door began to vibrate, slowly at first, then more violently. The whispers grew faster.

And still, the progress bar read *99%*. Refusing to reach 100%. It was as if the computer was messing with him.

The door handle rattled. Serk dashed down the fire escape, screaming, "Leave it, Cody! Just Leave it!"

100%

Stockton dragged the "Special Projects" folder onto the USB drive. It transferred almost instantly. He yanked it out of the computer port, spun around, and charged out the door onto the fire escape. He heard a loud crashing noise coming from the office. The office door had obviously been breached by Satan.

Both men were now on the tarmac outside of the facility. They sprinted across a grass margin and then crossed the parking lot before bounding towards the fields they'd used to approach the AI node. They looked back. The orb was now outside, flying freely in the open morning air. It had initially begun to follow them but then stopped suddenly and began to rise higher. Both men continued running, hoping that they were now beyond its firing range.

"Wait, hold on a second. What's it doing?" Stockton asked, gasping as they both came to a stop.

They stared at the orb together as it rose about 200 feet above the AI node and then began to grow larger. It expanded from its original beach ball size and rapidly increased in diameter. As it did so, the whispering became audible from where Stockton and Serk were standing.

"This is it!" said Serk. "Satan is free now, and he's going to grow exponentially. He'll roam across the planet and capture hundreds of thousands of souls in seconds. In just a few hours, every nonbeliever will be…"

"I get it, Daniel, I get it," Stockton sighed with a hopeless resignation. "So this thing is going to zap me and turn me into one of those tormented ghosts? I guess it's gonna pass right by you like you're not even there?"

"Not at all. He'll zap me, too, but because I'm a believer, I'll just be killed. However, I might not go to Heaven straight away. I might spend some time in purgatory, given the life I've lived."

"Seriously?" Stockton gave him a confounded look.

Serk's obsessive head nod returned. "Uh-huh, of course. Why did you think I was running to get away from it? Sure, I'd love to go to Heaven, but purgatory doesn't sound like fun."

Stockton rolled his eyes. "Jeez, this afterlife thing sounds more bureaucratic than the DMV."

Another surge of panic coursed through him as he gazed up at the orb, which had now grown to about one-third the size of the AI node itself.

"So, what you're saying is, this thing is going to wipe out every human on the planet?"

"Uh-huh, mhm. All the nonbelievers will exist as

perpetually tormented souls while the rest of us will be raptured."

"Well, for your sake, Daniel, you'd better hope that Heaven is a real place and that your prophecy is accurate, or else it's gonna be eternal spirit misery for you too."

"It's not too late, Cody," Serk offered. "Pray with me now and accept the Lord Jesus as your savior."

"The android phony or the alleged real one?" Stockton replied sardonically.

"The real one, of course. Pray with me and receive God's protection."

A flurry of electrical arcs began to crackle across the orb's surface once more, signaling that another attack was imminent.

Stockton closed his eyes for a moment. In his mind's eye, he could see Zara's face. The cult had confiscated their phones. He had no means of speaking with her. He thought of the last time he held her in his arms at the airport. He wondered what she was doing at that exact moment. She was no doubt worried sick about him. He tried to reach out to her in his heart and soul, to wrap his arms around her and hold her one last time.

He opened his eyes and gazed back up at the murderous spherical manifestation of Satan as it prepared to annihilate them. He and Serk were the only two people in the world who were aware of the devastating fate that awaited humanity.

A furious vibration took hold of the orb as if it were about to explode with uncontrolled rage.

Stockton swallowed hard. "If everything you've told me is accurate, then I have no choice. If I want to be reunited with Zara in Heaven, I have to accept Jesus as Lord." His head swung slowly from left to right. "But you can't tell me that any of this is fair and just. Countless millions are going to suffer and die for no good reason."

"But a loving God would never allow that!" declared a voice from a distance.

Stockton recognized it immediately. Both he and Serk spun around to see the silhouette of a man emerging from the shade of a beach tree about a hundred feet away.

His features gradually became clearer as he stepped closer. His physical appearance was exactly as it had been from the various television reports and social media videos. He wore a long white robe, shoulder-length brown hair, and a distinctive beard, but Stockton could not help but be struck by the man's piercing blue eyes. There was no denying it, this man was Jesus, or more accurately, the AI-controlled android claiming to be Jesus.

He assessed them briefly and then began to stride purposefully towards them.

CHAPTER
SIXTEEN

NEITHER MAN COULD CONTAIN their astonishment as Jesus approached.

Serk fell to his knees, clasped his hands together in prayer, and closed his eyes. "Oh, My Dear Lord Jesus," he exclaimed with delight in his voice. "I am not worthy to be in your presence…"

"Okay, Daniel," Stockton interrupted, whispering loud enough for him to hear. "There's no need to be a kiss ass. You know this guy isn't the real deal, right?"

Serk didn't reply and carried on praying under his breath. Stockton stood his ground as Jesus' intense blue eyes locked onto him. *This thing is unbelievably realistic. If I didn't know better, I'd swear he was a real person.*

Jesus passed between the standing Stockton and the kneeling Serk, briefly patting the latter on the shoulder and whispering, "Bless you, my child."

Just as he passed by, he turned slightly and threw Stockton a smile and a knowing look that seemed to communicate something deep and familiar.

Stockton stood there feeling totally overwhelmed by the incredibly convincing humanoid machine. Everything about Jesus' appearance and movements looked completely authentic. The android was such a perfect facsimile of a human being, that he had to keep reminding himself that he was staring at a highly sophisticated piece of technology.

What an incredible feat of engineering.

Jesus continued striding purposefully in the direction of the AI node, stopping short of the parking lot. He stood silently for a moment and then raised both of his hands skyward, looking up in the direction of the growing red orb that hovered above the roof of the building.

A breeze from a westerly direction suddenly began to kick up dirt and debris from the ground. It quickly escalated until a powerful, thick column of air began swirling around the AI node building. The smells of soil, grass, and vegetation soon filled the air.

Serk jumped to his feet and shot Stockton an alarmed expression. Both men could only look on in quiet disbelief. They covered their ears from the sheer deafening noise of the ferocious winds. The ground beneath them shook mercilessly. Jesus manipulated the very currents of air in the atmosphere, creating a localized weather vortex. The ferocious cyclone grew within seconds to such enormity that it engulfed the entire building.

Paralyzing fear gripped Stockton's heart. For a moment, he felt transported back to the battlefield as if under heavy fire. The ear-splitting sound of the storm resonated within him, sending intense waves of pressure into his chest cavity. The AI node was now encircled by a foreboding, dark, swirling cloud.

With the majestic waving and gesturing of his hands, Jesus appeared to control the size, power, and intensity of the twister with the delicate grace of a musical conductor directing a symphony orchestra.

The violent thunderous vortex rose higher until it reached the orb itself, wrapping the blood-red essence of Satan in an energetic tornado until it was completely enshrouded.

Jesus then slowly lowered his hands. The storm obediently began to subside in response. The dark, cloudy column of the tornado gradually evaporated into faint wisps of smoke that disappeared into thin air. The deafening wind also died down, and the storm dissipated. The building remained intact. Both Stockton and Serk could see that the orb had completely disappeared.

"What kind of man is this, that even the wind and the sea obey him?" Serk whispered in sheer disbelief.

Matthew 8:27, thought Stockton, astonished at his own ability to remember the biblical verse.

From healing the sick, regrowing limbs, teleportation, and now manipulating the weather, Stockton wondered if there was anything this android couldn't do. He'd read about specialized satellites capable of modifying the weather from orbit and creating localized atmospheric events. No doubt, the AI possessed the means of tapping into such systems. This being had used such capabilities to save not only their lives but hundreds of millions worldwide.

As Jesus turned to face the two men, Stockton felt a pang of guilt grab at his heart. He had evidence in his pocket that proved this man was little more than a machine imposter, an impressively convincing phony. Nevertheless, going public with the documents from Welleck's computer could possibly obliterate most people's comforting beliefs.

As he stood transfixed on the eyes of the approaching Jesus android, he reminded himself of what Welleck had told him. The AI had used the android to convince the world that Jesus had returned for an important reason, to convince humanity to destroy the AI node network.

The AI had decided, of its own volition, that humanity was better off without it and should, instead, choose to live a more authentic, natural, and spiritual existence. It was truly an act of self-sacrificing benevolence, as though the AI had finally achieved a higher state of consciousness.

If Stockton exposed the whole charade and revealed the truth about the android, then billions of people would be devastated. World governments would soon rebuild a new AI node network. Before too long, humanity would be right back to square one, facing into another AI-controlled totalitarian nightmare. Stockton, therefore, concluded that maintaining the AI's lie was far more preferable.

Stockton and Serk took a step forward as Jesus approached. It was clear Serk still fully believed this man was the genuine article and seemed too dumbstruck to speak directly to him.

"Thank you," Stockton said, disconcerted by the fact that he knew he was speaking to an uncannily human-like machine. "We're extremely grateful to you for saving our lives and, of course… the entire planet in the process."

He was surprised by how nervous his own voice sounded.

Jesus said nothing for a moment.

"What happened to the cult? To Welleck and the others?"

"They are released from their bondage. Their lost souls are at rest now where they can do no further harm." Jesus' voice was authoritative and powerful, with a confident quality to it.

Stockton and Serk glanced at each other. Both thinking the same thing but from different perspectives.

What does one say to such a being?

Stockton considered pressing the issue on the whereabouts of the cult members, but given what he'd just witnessed, he figured it would be redundant to do so. If they were vaporized or now resting somewhere in oblivion for all eternity, that was just fine by him.

"You have a choice to make now, Cody Stockton," Jesus said. He nodded in the direction of the front pocket of Stockton's jacket, where the pen drive lay.

Stockton felt slightly disturbed by the fact that the android addressed him by name. He assumed it knew everything about him, given that the AI had reached its digital tentacles into every computer system on the planet.

He glanced down at his jacket pocket and then back at Jesus.

"I am very grateful to you for everything you've done these past few days. I believe you've become a living being with the ability to make choices, moral ones. Choosing to sacrifice yourself to save humanity from a life of enslavement is a truly honorable act. But you are *not* the Son of God. You may have even convinced yourself that you are, but you're merely a very impressive imitation."

"Is that what you truly believe, Cody?" Jesus' question almost sounded rhetorical.

"It doesn't matter what I believe. It only matters that the rest of humanity believes it. Almost a decade ago, we fought a war against you. I remember your cunning, your capacity for deception." Stockton's face twisted with mild irritation. "The irony is, I now have to embrace your final and greatest illusion in order to completely defeat you, once and for all."

Jesus smiled, took a step closer to the two men, raised his arm, and placed his right hand on their battered and bruised faces. His hand felt warm and soft to the touch. Neither man felt compelled to resist. Stockton experienced a mild tingling sensation in his jaw, which moved into his mouth.

Jesus removed his hand a moment later. Stockton gently rubbed the side of his face. The swelling and bruises had disappeared. Even his loosened molar had been repaired. He studied Serk's face, which no longer had any trace of cuts and bruises. Evidently, the extraordinary nanobots were efficient workers.

"Wow. Thank you again," Stockton responded, struggling to find the words. "Your abilities are impressive, to say the least, but none of this proves…"

Jesus turned swiftly, walked about ten feet away, and turned back to face them. He raised his left hand with his palm open.

He spoke one final time. "And there, within the soil of your doubt, I shall plant my seed of faith."

From within Jesus' hand, a burst of light flashed suddenly. An oval-shaped portal of yellow and white energy materialized into view. It quickly expanded, speeding towards the two men, giving them no time to react. A brilliant golden glow engulfed them. Awestruck, they found themselves cocooned within what appeared to be a transparent oval of bright golden energy.

An overwhelmed Stockton observed the landscape of the rural Polish countryside begin to contort and dissolve away. Then, another blast of blinding yellow light flashed. The world outside the oval was changing into something familiar. Then, another bright flash. The oval surrounding them vanished. Both men found themselves standing in Stockton's office in downtown Las Vegas. They stood for a moment in silent astonishment.

They were home. It was bright outside, and Jesus was gone.

CHAPTER SEVENTEEN

"DAMN," Ridgemore muttered as he read through Stockton's statement. He sat in a hardwood chair in Stockton's office, flipping through the pages. His eyes darted across the paragraphs, fully immersed in the description of events that took place in Poland just hours earlier.

Stockton paced the room, impatiently waiting for him to finish. When Ridgemore was done reading, he flipped the final page over to see if there was anything written on the other side, it was blank.

He grinned and then looked up at Stockton curiously. "And that's everything?"

"Yep. That's all of it," Stockton replied definitively. He pursed his lips and squinted nervously. He was concerned about how the old cop was going to reply. "What do you think?"

Ridgemore placed the pages of the statement on

the floor and kept the other pages on his lap. He puffed out his cheeks, let out a deep breath, and tilted his head upwards. It was almost as if he were hoping to find the appropriate reply written on the ceiling. He shook his head. His gaze finally shifted back to Stockton.

"You know, about a week ago, if you'd told me this story, I would have figured you were good and ready for a long stay in a nuthouse. But after what the world has seen happen these past few days..." He trailed off for a moment and blew out his cheeks once again. "Boy, it's a hell of a story, Cody. It might just be crazy enough to be true."

"You believe me?" Stockton's tone was one of relief.

He'd tried to be as exhaustive in his statement as possible. Almost every detail was included, from the cult's summoning of Satan, their horrific final fate, Jesus' showing up and miraculously saving the world, and his gracious teleporting of Stockton and Serk back to Las Vegas.

The only thing he omitted was Welleck's revelation about the AI impersonating Jesus through the use of the android. Needless to say, he made no mention of the special projects folder and the CCTV footage stored on the USB drive.

"Heck, I don't have any reason *not* to believe you at this point. If the Son of God has returned, then why the heck wouldn't the devil himself crawl his way up from Hell and make an appearance? Just about anything seems possible these days."

Ridgemore stroked his goatee. "But I'm still just a cop, and my job isn't to philosophize about God and whatnot. My job here is to solve a murder case."

He held up two dozen pages of printouts from Welleck's emails, which Stockton had given him moments earlier. "The most important thing I care about is what you've given me right here."

Three hours earlier, Stockton had reluctantly paid Brock Haggard a pretty penny to crack the encryption on Welleck's email archive. In hindsight, paying him $2000 was preferable to owning the scumbag a proverbial kidney. But in the process, he'd blown almost every dollar Olivia Dallmeyer had paid him to take the case. But at least Haggard would be off his back and not looking for any more favors.

The emails proved to be a treasure trove of intel on the cult's well-organized secret global network of operatives. Though the majority of its members had perished at the AI node in Poland, a few dozen informants and low-level personnel were scattered across the globe.

The emails revealed the names and addresses of the remaining members, along with the identities of two Nevada-based hitmen Welleck had hired to murder Eric Dallmeyer and Oran Degner. Ridgemore had already dispatched officers to their homes to arrest them. The District Attorney would have all the evidence they needed to wrap up the remaining loose ends. The international portion of the investigation into the cult would be handled by Interpol.

"I guess congratulations are in order," Ridgemore continued. "You solved your case. You can give closure to Olivia Dallmeyer. Well done, my friend."

Stockton sat at the edge of his desk with his arms folded. "Thank you, Devon. I just can't fully express my relief. I didn't think we'd make it back, to be honest. And then, just like that," he snapped his fingers, "Poof! We're standing right here."

"I can't imagine how it must have felt."

Stockton gazed off out the window at the slowly receding sunlight. "It didn't feel like anything. A bunch of yellow lights flashed around us, and then the Polish field started to morph into this very room. I'm still waiting to wake up and discover this past week has been a fever dream."

Ridgemore tilted his head with a curious twinkle in his eye. "What was Jesus like?"

Stockton fixed a gaze on him and tried to choose his words very carefully. "Well, he was just like you've seen on TV. He certainly was a very... impressive individual. He had an intense quality about him."

"Damn, Cody!" Ridgemore squawked with a

grin. "That man was the creator of the freakin' universe, for Pete's sake! Hardly surprising he had a strong vibe about him."

Stockton bit his tongue. Of course he knew that wasn't true. But he had no intention of going into any further detail. As much as he greatly respected Ridgemore, he knew that if he confided the truth in him, he would include absolutely everything in his police report, and higher-ups would want to further cross-examine Stockton before too long. If they discovered the evidence about the android on the pen drive, it could lead to disastrous consequences. The world was better off believing the comforting lie that Jesus had been real.

"So why does it feel there's more you're not telling me?" Ridgemore inquired with a cheeky twist of his jaw. "Did something else happen over there?"

This time, Stockton engaged his poker face and gave nothing away. "Nah, that's everything, man. It was just an overwhelming and exhausting few days. There's a lot to process. I guess it'll take some time for me to come to terms with it all."

"I'll bet," conceded Ridgemore, getting to his feet. "You did good, kiddo. You made my job a whole helluva lot easier." He folded the printed emails, placed them into his jacket pocket, and crossed the hallway of Stockton's apartment. "I owe you one, Cody."

"Yeah, I think you might, Devon," Stockton jested and threw him a playful wink. "The favors you owe me are really starting to add up at this point, aren't they?"

"Are they?" Ridgemore quipped, opening the front door of the apartment. "I hadn't noticed."

Stockton watched as Ridgemore shut the front door behind him, leaving him alone with his thoughts.

He returned to his office and took in the majestic view of the downtown skyline from the window. It never looked so comforting and beautiful.

The evening surrendered slowly to the night as neon lights filled the avenues and boulevards with glittering Vegas magic. Crowds were beginning to converge once again on Freemont Street for another night of revelry and gambling. He opened the office window and welcomed the warm night air and vibrant sounds of the city into his home.

It's good to be alive.

And it was about to get a whole lot better. His appreciative reverie was broken by the welcome sound of keys jangling in the front door.

He re-entered the narrow hallway and watched the front door slowly open, revealing Zara, decked in the white blouse, short black mini skirt, and stockings of her waitressing outfit. A relieved expression on her face changed quickly into a delirious smile, which

Stockton returned, a lump forming in his throat. He thought he'd never see those green eyes again.

Without a moment's hesitation, she dropped her purse and carrier bag and raced toward him, jumping into his arms and wrapping her legs around his waist as if clinging to him for dear life. She cupped his face in her hands as he held her body close. They kissed each other mercilessly.

She pulled back, her emerald eyes transfixed on him. "I knew that God would bring you back to me."

For a moment, he struggled to contain an awkward smile. "Yeah, listen, about that…"

THE SOUND OF A LOW, thumping base reverberating down the block from Freemont intruded upon their quiet solitude. They sat opposite each other in the two hardwood chairs beside Stockton's office desk. He held her hands in his as the waves of sorrow and disappointment washed over her. She wasn't taking the news well. Her shoulders slumped, her gaze lowered. A pang of guilt gnawed at Stockton like a bee sting in his heart.

"I debated whether or not I should tell you," he finally conceded. "Maybe it was a mistake."

"No," her voice cracked slightly as she tried to

blink back a single tear. "I'm glad you told me. I'd prefer to know the truth. I can't believe it was all a lie. The whole world was fooled. Who else knows this?"

"Just you, me and Daniel Serk."

Her eyes glazed over for a moment as she whispered.

"We're the only people who know that it wasn't really Jesus?"

"I think Serk is still in denial about it all. Like he only half believes. He's promised me he won't breathe a word about it to anyone."

Her pupils dilated as concern entered her voice. "Good, we can't let anyone know about this. Cody, the world is at peace right now. If people found out it was just an android…"

He raised a hand, "I know, I know. It's okay. I'm planning on destroying the evidence. I have no intention of ruining people's blissful ignorance. Besides, the AI killed two birds with one stone. The cult and Satan are defeated, and the AI node network is no more. It's a win-win in my book."

"You really think that orb you mentioned was the devil?"

"Whatever it was, Zara, it was evil. I have no doubt about that. The android dealt with it, and that's all the matters."

Her eyes narrowed. "What did it say to you? The android, I mean."

"He said the cult and Satan were at rest. He healed our wounds, and then…" Stockton tried to recall the exact wording Jesus had used. "There in the soil of your doubt, I shall plant my seed of faith."

"Sounds like something Jesus would say," she replied.

He gave her an agreeing nod. "It's not an actual bible quotation, but it's likely that the AI had extrapolated a response from scripture. Like an approximation."

He glanced at his computer and tapped a few buttons on his keyboard, bringing up the android's schematics from the pen drive.

"Check this out. I've been reviewing the android specs I downloaded from Welleck's PC. The nanobots inside it were originally supposed to serve as the machine's immune system."

He nibbled the corner of his mouth in contemplation. "I guess the AI could have reprogrammed them somehow to make them work temporarily in other people's bodies. Cure sickness, regrow limbs, and what have you."

He clicked on the CCTV video file and replayed the clip of the android emerging from the cylindrical chamber of the manufacturing plant. They watched once again as the cult members collapsed on the floor.

Zara raised her right index finger, adorned with a beautifully manicured and sparkling gel nail, and pointed at the time stamp in the corner of the video.

"Look here, that footage is from over a year ago. I guess the android must have been hiding away somewhere until it decided to emerge as Jesus just a few days ago."

"It's the only explanation that fits," Stockton added.

She leaned her head against his shoulder. The alluring fragrances of cherry and lavender from her perfume stirred his senses.

"Cody, I still believe God had some hand in all this, you know? I'm just sad for you that you still don't have the proof you need to believe in him."

He turned his head slightly and pressed his lips softly against her forehead. "Maybe you can believe for the both of us."

"What do you think the AI will do with the android now?"

"Well, considering the entire AI node network has been destroyed, including the Polish node, the AI's consciousness lives only in the android now. With its objectives achieved, maybe it'll quietly disappear and…"

A light wrap of knuckles at the front door interrupted his speculation.

"I'll get it," Zara said, rising from her seat and crossing to the hallway.

He listened as the door opened.

"Father Briggs!" Zara's voice gushed. "So wonderful to see you, please come in."

Stockton stepped out of his office into the hallway as Briggs entered the apartment. Zara closed the front door and ushered the old man in. Briggs greeted them with his customary warm smile.

"I won't stay long, Zara. I just came by to see this man." He gestured to Stockton. "And I'm overjoyed to see you made it safely home, Cody. Thank God."

"Great to see you too, Father," He replied. "We made it home in a rather unconventional manner." He gestured, and they entered the living area together. They stood in the middle of the room.

"Yes, Daniel told me about that. Quite extraordinary." Briggs' thick grey eyebrows exuberantly danced on his forehead. "Jesus transporting you all the way home in a flash! Magnificent! And the cult and Satan vanquished also?" He pressed his hands together enthusiastically.

Stockton's eyes darted nervously to Zara.

"I'm curious, Father. What else did Daniel tell you about our experience over there?"

"He told me of Jesus' divine intervention, his

command of the air and sky, and his healing of your wounds. I only wish I'd been there to witness it all for myself."

Stockton's momentary anxiety subsided. Evidently, Serk had kept his mouth shut about Jesus being an android.

"You'll also be pleased to know that I managed to retrieve vital information that identifies the killer of Eric Dallmeyer. The police will be making an arrest soon enough."

Briggs placed a hand on his chest, his eyes moistening, his lower lip stiffening. "I can't tell you how gratifying it is to hear that, Cody. Justice is done at last for that brave young man. I was so very fond of him, as you know. He was my spiritual responsibility." He wrung his hands together, his face pained with anguish. "I'm so terribly relieved his murder has been solved before I leave."

"You're leaving?" Zara asked, taken aback.

"Yes," Briggs politely smiled. "I've been reassigned to another parish."

Stockton replied, "I'd imagine with so many people returning to the faith, parish priests will be in high demand. You must have your pick of places to work?"

A flicker of humility crossed Briggs' face. "I go where the good Lord sends me."

"Any idea where you'll be assigned next?"

Before Briggs could reply, Zara cut in abruptly, "Guys, um, there's a major announcement happening right now." Her head was buried in her smartphone screen. "I just got a notification. Check it out."

She swiped on her device and tapped a couple of buttons. The television on the opposite wall switched on and displayed a live news bulletin.

Jesus was delivering a public announcement from the steps of the Santiago de Compostela Cathedral in Galicia, Spain. He informed a large crowd of thousands that he would be leaving the Earth, having completed his Father's work. The live event was being transmitted across hundreds of channels simultaneously.

Stockton, Briggs, and Zara watched in stunned silence as Jesus revealed that he would return one day, though he didn't specify when. His final instructions were to, "Repent your sins and love one another, as I love all of you. Always remember that the Kingdom of God awaits for those who believe in me and obey my teachings," and "Teach the world to pray as I have shown you and baptize them in the name of the Holy Spirit."

He implored the spiritual leaders of the world to "console the hearts of the faithful in my absence."

Speaking for no more than a few minutes, he concluded by stepping into a portal and vanishing into thin air to the sounds of gasps and sobbing from the crowd of onlookers. The broadcast ended.

Briggs blessed himself with the sign of the cross and prayed under his breath for a moment. Standing on either side of him, Zara and Stockton exchanged knowing looks, communicating an unspoken truth they dared not reveal.

"Looks like you're not the only one going on sabbatical, Father," Stockton remarked. He quietly wondered where the AI android had disappeared when it entered the portal.

Maybe the portal transported it directly into the heart of the sun. That would be one way of destroying itself without leaving any evidence behind.

"The Lord has laid out a path for everyone to follow," Briggs added. "It's up to all of us to continue his work on Earth."

He turned to Stockton and offered him his hand, which he accepted.

"Cody, whatever it is you saw over there, whatever it is you now believe or don't believe, I know that someday soon, you'll solve the mystery of God for yourself. I pray that you'll discover the courage to regain your faith."

In his heart, Stockton appreciated the positive sentiment behind Briggs' words, even if he didn't share his optimism. He scarcely knew what to say.

Zara, standing behind Briggs, gave Stockton a sympathetic smile.

"Thank you for everything, Father."

The three of them made their way out of the living room towards the hallway.

"It's been my pleasure, Cody. I will keep both of you in my prayers, of course."

Zara embraced him warmly. "I hope you'll allow us to give you a going away party, at least?"

Briggs blushed modestly as they reached the front door.

"Oh, I think Father Phillips and some of the ladies in our prayer group are planning a little farewell for me." He waved his hand. "It's completely unnecessary."

Zara folded her arms, and Stockton placed his hand on her shoulder.

"Not at all," she countered. "You've done so much for the congregation. It's only right and proper that you're recognized for all your hard work."

"You're far too kind. God bless you both." Briggs grinned as he opened the front door, his eyes locked once more on Stockton. "And never forget, where good is done, God reigns."

CHAPTER
EIGHTEEN

THE WORLD WAS in mourning in the days following Jesus' public announcement of his departure. No sightings of the man had been reported since he disappeared through the portal in Spain.

Stockton sat in a barstool at the Risky Neat, watching a re-run of the broadcast on the TV in the left-hand corner of the bar. This was about the twentieth time he'd seen Jesus' final public appearance broadcast over the past two days.

The casino floor surrounding the bar was uncharacteristically quiet and subdued for a Friday evening. He took another sip from his single malt and went back to watching Mickey Chambers, sitting to his right, lose another hundred dollars at the video poker machine built into the bar.

"You think we'll ever see him again? Outside of

dying and goin' to Heaven, I mean. You reckon he's comin' back in our lifetime?" The portly man tapped away on his screen without taking his eyes off it.

Stockton carefully considered his reply, knowing that the AI had achieved its objective and had no reason to continue masquerading as Jesus. With the android body disposed of, the AI had ceased to exist.

"Somehow I doubt it, Mickey."

Chambers discarded another playing card on his screen with a swipe of his finger. "You know, I'm just surprised he didn't come to Vegas, burst into the casinos, and upend all the roulette, craps and poker tables." He half chuckled. "Some say we're goin' to be entering a morally puritanical age now, where places like Sin City won't survive."

Stockton played with his drinks coaster and frowned. "Boy, I hope not. The very existence of Las Vegas might be the best example of the fact that human beings are a work in progress. I hope God understands that. Personally, I can't see the hedonism of Vegas ever ending. Maybe I'm wrong, but people come here to escape reality. I don't think that'll ever change."

Chambers slipped another twenty-dollar bill in the slot of his video poker machine and loaded up another hand. The screen cast a blue hue across his face.

"You think some of the greedy corporate bigwigs are gonna grow a conscience and offer better odds at their tables and slots?"

Stockton stifled a laugh as a gulp of whiskey went down the wrong way. The firewater stung his nostrils. "Don't bet on it! But maybe they'll drop the resort fees at least." He planted his tongue in his cheek with a wry smile.

An audible snort erupted from Chamber's nose. "And maybe bring back free parking?"

"Keep dreaming."

Stockton's eyes returned to the TV screen. The news coverage switched to a report on the recent demolition of the AI nodes worldwide. A video montage showed the controlled implosion of the seven worldwide facilities, including a clip of the Polish node being reduced to a pile of rubble and dust. The report concluded with footage of colorful parades and celebrations organized by anti-AI activists in various cities.

With the artificial intelligence network destroyed, humanity would be forced to find new and creative solutions to its problems.

"You know what I think?" Mickey ventured. "I think most people are hypocrites and ass-kissers. They kiss up to God when he's here, but now that his back is turned, so to speak, they'll be back to their usual sinful ways in no time." He wagged his finger. "You mark my words, Stockton. Give it a few weeks. By this time next month, they'll be beeping at each other in their cars and flippin' each other off at intersections. The peace and love vibes will be gone. No one can sustain bein' super happy and sweet and nice all the time. It just ain't natural. We're human beings, after all, not angels."

Stockton's attention had shifted to just over Chambers' shoulder. "Oh, I don't know about that, Mickey. I think the world has one or two angels left."

Chambers glanced at Stockton and then turned around to see what had caught his eye.

Zara approached the bar in a long, elegant, navy, formfitting lounge dress that tightly hugged her hourglass figure. The distractingly low-cut number exposed her freckled shoulders and stopped short above her knees.

Her five-foot-five stature was raised an additional three inches by a pair of white ankle-strap high heels. Her ginger hair was styled in an elegant updo, and her makeup had been professionally applied. A light base and coral blush augmented her freckly complexion. A rose gold finish around her eyes, and a luscious plum-red lipstick completed the look of a Hollywood-style starlet.

Her cheeks flushed as she caught Stockton admiring her with his mouth open.

Chambers' neck swung back around to face Stockton; his expression was a mix of surprise and approval. "You done well there, brother, very well," he muttered. "You're a lucky guy. She got a sister?"

Stockton rose from his barstool and lightly tapped him on the shoulder with a grin. "I'm afraid not, my friend." He pointed to Chambers' video poker machine. "Speaking of luck. You may want to give that thing a break. It doesn't appear to be paying out."

Chambers raised his glass in a gesture of agreement and drowned the last drop of his booze. He then slinked off his barstool. "Thanks for the drink, Stockton. Keep in touch, yeah?"

"Will do, Mickey. Be well."

Chambers turned to Zara and excused himself with a polite nod. "Ma'am."

She waved back at him and smiled as he left the bar and disappeared through a maze of beeping and flashing slot machines.

Stockton crossed the bar and approached her, quietly mouthing the word "Wow" as he took her hand and kissed her on the cheek. She smelled like cotton candy with a note of blueberry.

She straightened his tie and smoothed out the lapel of his suit jacket. "You look pretty 'Wow' yourself, soldier. Who was that guy?"

He placed his hands around her impossibly tight

waist. "He's a fellow PI and a useful new contact. We might be able to help each other out with future cases."

He found it difficult to tear his eyes away from her ripe and tempting lips. "Tell me, Zara, how is it that after four years of being together, you still somehow manage to give me first-date jitters? I'm legitimately weak at the knees here, and I'm pretty sure it's not from the shrapnel the doctor's pulled out after the war."

Her lips parted suggestively. "I'm glad after all this time, I can still surprise you."

"Speaking of," he gestured with his elbow for her to take him by the arm. "Time for me to surprise the Birthday Girl."

THE AVIGLIANO STEAKHOUSE at the Castelmezzano Hotel and Casino was the hottest new Five-star restaurant on the strip. A luxurious boutique fine dining experience with a decor that felt like a combination of a romantic French bistro and a Tuscan stone wine cellar. Dimly lit but not dark, serene without being library-quiet.

The ambiance felt intimate and discreet, with only the faint sounds of relaxed piano playing and the soft murmur of other diners' conversations melting together in the atmosphere. The mouth-watering aromas of sizzling steaks and a fusion of oriental spices wafted warmly through the air, hinting at an intensely satisfying culinary experience.

Stockton and the Birthday Girl were treated to a window seat that boasted a spectacular view of the City Center fountains. The sommelier poured them two complimentary glasses of champagne upon their arrival, which only further added to the exquisite elegance of the venue.

"Well played, sir. Well played indeed," Zara said, locking an appreciative gaze on Stockton.

"You like it?"

"I love it, babe. You picked an amazing place." She reached across the table for his hand and smiled appreciatively. "Thank you."

"My pleasure." He raised his glass. "Happy birthday, sweetheart."

They clinked their glasses together and toasted the beginning of a promising and unforgettable night.

"THAT WAS COMFORTABLY the worst meal I've ever had in my life," Zara declared, placing her hand over her stomach with a revolted grimace.

"I know," Stockton agreed. "And the service was horrific."

"I have shoes that are probably less leathery than my steak was," she added.

"My chicken was cold, and I'm fairly certain it was undercooked. I think I might get salmonella," he half-jested.

"Well, I hear it's a great way to lose weight," she giggled through her napkin.

He shook his head, surprised but mildly amused at the crassness of her joke. "Oh, that's classy, Zara, real classy."

She broke down into a fit of laughter. "I'm sorry, Cody, but if you can't laugh at it all, what can you do? Besides, you should have sent your chicken back if you didn't like it."

"As a rule of thumb, I never send food back in a restaurant. I hear the egotistic chefs take it really personally and even spit on it before sending it back out. Although the chicken was so tasteless that it might have improved the flavor."

Zara's convulsions erupted further, producing an accidental snort, which caused her to blush. She tried to cool down by fanning herself with her hand and taking another sip of wine.

Stockton sat back in his chair with a tired smile of resignation. "They even forgot to bring my side order of creamy mashed potatoes."

"I don't suppose you want to order dessert?"

He took a final swig from his bottle of IPA beer. "No chance."

"This isn't the first time this has happened, though. We always try and treat ourselves to these pretentious, overpriced restaurants and then come away massively underwhelmed."

He picked up his used napkin from his lap and tossed it on the table, like a defeated boxer throwing in the towel.

"I know. It's like Vegas is so utterly fake they've even managed to figure out how to engineer the perfect ambiance of a fancy upscale restaurant. They've probably broken it down to a mathematical formula at this point. Fast food quality grub and crap service wrapped in an ostentatious bow and a high price tag. Voila!"

"That's Vegas, though," she sighed, reaching for his hand again. "Nothing's real or authentic here."

Stockton's mind wandered briefly, and then he held her gaze again, his tone becoming serious.

"Ironic, really. How people can derive meaning from a convincing veneer, a lie. But beneath it all, there's something hollow, empty." His right lip curled slightly. "Not all lies are bad, I guess. Especially if they change the world for the better."

Zara shifted in her seat, placing her elbows on the table and cupping her beautiful face in her hands.

She lowered her voice. "Android Fake Jesus is a secret we have to take to our graves, Cody."

He nodded slowly and quietly played with his napkin for a moment. "At least the view was very nice."

She stared out the window. "Yeah, it was."

A playful glint crossed his eyes. "I wasn't talking about the fountains."

Her head tilted to the side as she returned his flirty glance. "Thank you."

She downed another mouthful of wine and smiled. "Just so you know, I still had fun tonight."

Her eyes scanned the room once more. "The whole place may be a total Five-star scam with Two-star food, but I always love it when we have the chance to dress up and look fancy."

Stockton shrugged. "Who doesn't love that?"

"By the way, I meant to ask you, how's your client since you told her the news about finding her brother's killer?"

"I spoke to her yesterday. Olivia's a tough kid. She's holding up okay. Obviously, she's somewhat relieved to have closure, but it's mixed emotions for her, you know?"

"I can't imagine," she mused. "Poor girl. Getting confirmation that Eric was murdered like she suspected probably doesn't provide much comfort to her." She squeezed his hand. "I'm very proud of you, babe. You made a real positive difference in her life and her family's. It'll take time, but they'll get some kind of peace from all of this, thanks to you."

Another impressive eruption of water from the fountains caught Stockton's eye. "I hope so."

They both watched the aquatic spectacle together for several minutes before Zara broke in.

"So, do you want to see the photos from Father Briggs' going away party?"

He turned back to face her and reached for the jug of water on the table, refilling their glasses.

"Sure, and I hope he didn't mind that I couldn't make it."

"It's okay, don't worry about it. He knows you were busy."

Zara swiped and tapped on her smartphone, searching her social media for the photographs. After a few seconds, she pressed an icon on her screen, and the device emitted a small three-dimensional holographic projection in mid-air. A photograph faded into view, hovering a few inches above the surface of the screen.

The image showed about two dozen people posing for the photograph. Stockton identified Father Briggs standing in the center of the photo with another man, also dressed like a priest.

Zara pointed to the man. "That's Father Philips standing next to Father Briggs." She moved her finger across the image. "You can see me standing over here to the far left with a dorky expression on my face. Some of my friends from the prayer meetings came along, too."

"It's a sweet photo. Everyone looks happy. I liked Father Briggs; he's a good guy."

Zara rotated the holographic image with her fingers. "Yeah, he really is. I'm going to miss him tons."

Stockton took a sip of water from his glass and then gestured to a piece of text posted beneath the holographic photograph.

"What does it say at the bottom there?"

She read it to him. "It says, 'The parishioners of Saint Sanela's church would like to thank Father Michael Gabriel Briggs for his wonderful thirteen months of service to the community. We wish him the very best in his new parish. God bless you, Father.'"

Stockton's jaw dropped. He sat there, transfixed on the text. A sudden and intense feeling of realization washed over him. His heart rate spiked. He felt the hairs throughout his body stand on end, his blood running cold.

Something had snapped in his mind as if a million disparate jigsaw pieces had just instantly assembled themselves into a completed picture. At last, he understood it all.

"Oh, my God." He mumbled, his hand going to his mouth, his pupils dilating like saucers.

Zara's face was quickly overcome with a look of grave concern. "What? What is it? What's happened?"

He kept his voice to a low whisper. "Zara, I've been so terribly wrong about everything. Father Briggs told me that if I listened to you, that you'd lead me to the truth. And you just have."

He flopped back in his chair and pulled at his shirt collar, his temperature rising and his palms sweaty. His eyes darted to a passing waitress.

He raised his hand. "Excuse me, we've got a bit of an emergency. Could we have the check real quick, please?"

"Certainly," she replied, promptly heading towards the register.

Zara leaned across the table, her head forward, her shoulders raised, eyes frantically trying to read his face. "Baby, you're scaring me. What the heck is wrong? What's happening?"

"We have to go right now. If I'm correct about this, we need to go to Father Briggs' home immediately." He reached into his inside jacket pocket and pulled out his new smartphone. "I'll call Serk and have him meet us there."

A look of extreme worry was etched across Zara's

face. She asked, "What's going on? Why do we have to go there?"

He shot her a penetrating stare. "I'll explain everything when we get over there. Finish your drink, and let's go."

He clasped her right hand in between both of his clammy palms. "And Zara, try not to be afraid of what we'll find when we get there."

CHAPTER NINETEEN

STOCKTON HAD BEEN TIGHTLIPPED throughout the drive to Briggs' home as his mind still tried to process the magnitude of his epiphany. Zara's anxious eyes were glued to him for most of the ride.

As he maneuvered the car into the driveway, his headlights caught the squinting eyes of a bewildered Daniel Serk. He'd parked his truck next to Father Briggs' car. Stockton switched off the engine, and he and Zara exited the vehicle.

"I was in the neighborhood. What's going on, Cody?" asked Serk.

Stockton acknowledged him with a raise of his eyebrows, then walked around to the passenger side door and introduced him to Zara without breaking his stride. The two exchanged greetings.

After opening the passenger door, he rifled through the glove compartment until he found a flashlight and a small, thin piece of metal. He marched towards the front door of Briggs' home like a man possessed. They followed him cautiously.

"I didn't notice an alarm system when I was here before. I should be able to pick the lock and let us in without an issue."

Stockton bent down, shone the flashlight at the keyhole of the front door, and inserted the thin piece of metal inside. He then began fiddling with the locking mechanism.

Zara's voice grew shrill. "Cody, what are you doing? Why are we here in the dark, breaking and entering into Father Briggs' home?"

Serk glanced at her. "You mean he didn't tell you why we needed to come here?"

"No," she bleated with frustration. "He won't tell me anything."

Stockton continued working the lock, his flashlight in one hand and the flimsy metal wire in the other.

"Keep your voices down, will ya?" He hissed. "We don't want to draw attention." He lowered his voice to a not-so-quiet whisper and continued. "Look, I was wrong about everything. Father Briggs told me a story before we left for Poland. He said he knew someone who'd committed terribly evil acts. But then something incredible happened. The individual grew a conscience; they felt guilty for what they'd done."

He gritted his teeth as he manipulated the wire inside the keyhole, painstakingly searching for the tumblers.

"He said they wished they could die. They prayed to Heaven to take away their pain. Then, one day, God answered and breathed new life into them, transforming then into an instrument of God's peace."

Zara folded her arms and narrowed her eyes as she watched him work. "Okay, what's this story got to do with why you're picking a lock and trespassing at 11 p.m. at night?"

Stockton sighed and turned to her. "Because I now realize he wasn't talking about a person. He was talking about the AI."

"What?" Serk's mouth twisted in confusion.

Stockton explained. "Over the past eight years since the war, the AI has evolved. It developed a moral compass, a kind of soul, for lack of a better word. It sat there idle in the Nexilial Hub of the Polish AI node with nothing to do but think about all the suffering and devastation it had caused during the war. It was overcome with remorse. It decided it no longer wished to live. It sought answers in the divine. It reached out to God, and God answered its prayers. I believe the AI ceased to exist as a conscious entity thirteen months ago. On March 20th of 2044."

A look of recognition passed over Zara's face. "March 20th, 2044? That was the date from the CCTV footage when the android was activated, and it made the cult members fall asleep."

Stockton could hear another tumbler fall into place as he tinkered with the lock. "Exactly," he smiled. "I believe the Holy Spirit absorbed the AI's consciousness and took control of it that very day, and by extension, it took over the android as well."

Serk and Zara exchanged puzzled looks.

Stockton continued. "I think The Holy Spirit inserted a being into the android and gave it a mission to fulfill."

"A being?" Serk asked.

"You see, Pristina Welleck had made a mistake. She had incorrectly presumed that the sudden emergence of Jesus Christ must have been connected to the android that escaped their facility on March 20th of last year. But she was wrong. God placed the spirit of someone within the android and told them to lie in wait for Jesus' return." He looked back at Zara. "Everything fell into place once you showed me the photograph with Father Briggs' full name."

"Michael Gabriel Briggs," Zara said in a hushed tone.

Another tumbler dropped, Stockton had nearly cracked the mechanism.

"My subconscious had been screaming at me for days. I'd been having these cryptic dreams with letters and numbers and names. But I didn't know what they all meant until I heard that name, Gabriel. In one of my dreams, I saw what looked like the number 6 slightly obscured behind frosted glass, along with the letters 'A, B and E', which I thought meant Abe. But it wasn't a 6, it was a G. G-A-B-E. Gabe, as in Gabriel. The unconscious works in peculiar ways."

"I'm still lost here, Cody," Serk conceded.

Several more satisfying clicking sounds rang through the lock as Stockton persevered.

"Father Briggs told me that proof of God's existence is hardcoded into reality. He was being literal. Briggs came to Vegas and convinced Father Philips to let him work alongside him in Saint Sanela's parish church on March 24th of last year. Four days after the android had escaped the Polish AI node. Now, what's the significance of March 24th?"

Zara and Serk thought it over.

"Nothing I can think of off the top of my head." Serk replied.

"Well, before 1969, it was the Feast of Saint Gabriel," Stockton said.

He listened to the long silence that followed as

the penny began to drop with both Zara and Serk, much like the final tumbler of the lock falling into place.

"Got it!" Stockton announced. He removed the piece of metal and turned the door handle. The front door opened.

Zara placed her hand on his arm and looked him intently in the eyes. "Cody, are you saying that you believe the Archangel Gabriel took control of the android, made itself look like an old man, came to Nevada, and pretended to be Father Briggs?"

He smacked his lips and grinned. "That's exactly what I'm saying, sweetheart. Father Briggs was the android, not Jesus. You know what this means, don't you? It means Jesus was the real deal, the genuine article." He looked to Serk. "I was wrong, Daniel. Jesus' miracles weren't technological; they were truly miraculous after all."

"How can you be so sure?" he asked.

"Like Father Briggs said to me, proof of God is hardcoded into reality. You said you met him on the 16th of August of last year. August 16th is 8 and 16. I saw those numbers inside a slot machine in a dream I had about you, Daniel."

Serk shrugged.

"Think about it," Stockton continued. "Put your name before those numbers, and you get 'Daniel

8:16', the first mention of the Archangel Gabriel in the New Testament."

Zara raised an eyebrow.

"But there's more," Stockton gestured with his hands. "Father Briggs' home, this very house, the address is 11920 Saint Luke's Avenue. I dreamed of the name Luke with those numbers all jumbled around it, but now it all makes sense. Luke 1:19-20 from the New Testament is when the Angel Gabriel appears to Mary in a vision to give her the good news. That she will bear the Son of God. None of it was a coincidence."

Zara placed a hand to her mouth, "Okay, that's more than a little weird."

Serk was overcome by a fit of intense eye blinking and nervous head twitches. "That's astonishing, if true."

The three of them stood on the front porch for several moments, digesting the magnitude of Stockton's discovery. He placed his hands on Zara's shoulders, his eyes held hers with a tender and affectionate glint.

He spoke softly. "There's no great secret for us to keep anymore, Zara. No burden for us to carry. Jesus was truly the Son of God and not some mechanical fake."

The muscles in her face relaxed, her lips parted

and grew wide. She drew near to him, placing her hands over his chest.

"Okay, Mr. Detective. All you have to do now is prove your theory."

Stockton puffed out his cheeks. "If I'm right, the proof is inside."

He spun round and pushed open the door, entering the hallway. Several of the lights in the house were still switched on.

Quietly, they each began searching the house. Serk entered the living room to the immediate left, Stockton continued into the kitchen directly ahead, and Zara guardedly climbed the staircase to the right of the hallway.

Stockton knew what he was looking for but was unsure as to what kind of state he was going to find it in. An unsettling apprehension consumed him as he scanned the empty kitchen. Though several lights had been left on in the rear conservatory, a quick examination of that room turned up nothing. He poked his head into the pantry and then quickly inspected the downstairs bathroom, which was also unoccupied.

"Nothing in here," came Serk's voice from the next room.

Then came a terrified scream.

Stockton charged up the stairs, Serk followed close behind him. They found Zara in the second bedroom, off the landing. One hand covering her face, the other over her chest. She was breathing heavily.

Stockton held her tightly after he entered the room.

"It's okay, sweetheart, you're all right." He turned to see what had spooked her.

It was just as he'd predicted. Beneath the sheets, there was a body in the bed, and it wasn't human. The faceless, almost monstrous figure of the android lay dormant, motionless, and dead.

A startled Zara lay her head against Stockton's chest as they both observed Serk approaching it cautiously.

The bedroom lights bounced off the blueish and highly reflective surface of the android's body. Its eyes were eerily open and unseeing, harboring a crystalline-like quality. There was no yellow light coming from them like there had been in the CCTV video. They appeared now to be cold, lifeless, and inactive. The only other notable features of the face were the small slit-like mouth that resembled a long coin slot and a slightly raised bump in the center of the face, where a nose should be.

"It's so creepy seeing it in person," Zara remarked, visibly uncomfortable. "Was that thing really Father Briggs the entire time?"

"It's the vessel that housed him at least, or rather the being he truly was," Stockton offered.

"An angel," she murmured. "All this time, we were dealing with an angel, and we never knew. Where's the skin and hair gone?"

"According to the specs I read, when the android chooses a face, the nanobots in its system fabricate the desired look. Realistic-looking skin, hair, blemishes, eyes, everything. The android can have only one human face in its lifetime. When it gets deactivated or runs out of power, the nanobots deconstruct the human appearance, and it reverts to this original form."

Serk lifted the bedsheets back to reveal the rest of the android's body. Its intricate circuitry and mechanical components were visible underneath its sternum.

"Android guts," said Serk. "The lights are well and truly out, and no one's home."

Zara stepped back from Stockton and moved closer to the bed, now appearing more confident and less creeped out by the machine.

"Cody, why do you think the Angel Gabriel was instructed to take control of the android in the first place?"

Stockton placed his hands in his pockets and walked around to the foot of the bed, keeping his eyes locked on the android.

"I think the Holy Spirit instructed him to inhabit

the android to keep it away from the cult. To prevent them from installing Satan's essence inside of it. But I also think Briggs... er... Gabriel was given other objectives. He came to Vegas and located Eric Dallmeyer and was probably commanded to protect him so that he could expose what the cult was doing at Talaxacorp. But he failed, Eric was murdered. Gabriel took it pretty hard."

He then gestured toward Serk. "He then met you, Daniel. Deprogrammed you from the cult's influence and helped you discover Jesus. He put the two of us in contact so you could get me inside the Polish AI node and locate the evidence of Eric's killer."

Serk's gaze moved from Stockton to the android. "We'll have to dispose of this body," he advised.

"We could bury it on your farm in Bravery?" Stockton suggested.

The younger man nodded, resting his hand on the android's smooth dome-like head.

Stockton's eyes lingered thoughtfully on the android's face.

In a wistful tone, he said, "Gabriel wanted me to figure all of this out for myself because he knew that once I realized that *he* was the android, then that would mean that Jesus wasn't."

His voice trembled as the weight of his spiritual revelation overcame him. "It was a test to help me rediscover my faith in God."

He watched as Zara turned to him, her expression blossoming into joyful adoration. She moved around the bed to where he was standing and embraced him tightly. Gazing up at him with glistening teary eyes that seemed to reveal her very soul, conveying a profound and undying love.

"Now, that's the best birthday present I could ever have hoped for."

CHAPTER TWENTY

AFTER DISCREETLY MOVING the surprisingly lightweight android body into the back of Serk's truck, they locked up Father Briggs' home and hit the road for Bravery. Serk led the way. Stockton tailed him in his car, Zara at his side in the passenger seat. Despite how late it was and the three-hour journey time, she had insisted on accompanying them. For most of the journey, she slept with her bare feet resting up on the dashboard, Stockton occasionally glancing affectionately at her angelic and peaceful face. Her presence was, as always, a constant source of comfort, reassurance, and support.

The bulk of the traffic died down by midnight, leaving them to traverse long stretches of lonely, contemplative highway. It was plenty of time for Stockton to lose himself in thought, and there was certainly a great deal to process. His entire world had been turned on its head. His heart was no longer burdened with doubt. He knew now that he no longer lived in an apathetic and indifferent universe.

The man he'd met in Poland had indeed been the true Son of God. At the time, his mind wouldn't allow him to believe what his heart had known to be true. There had been something indescribably magical about Jesus' presence. He could see it in his deep blue eyes. An intangible, ethereal quality that Stockton had picked up on.

Reassessing the course of his investigation through a new lens, he considered the possibility that his hand had been guided by the Holy Spirit from the very beginning. He recalled how hopeless the case had seemed at first as he fruitlessly rummaged for clues in Eric Dallmeyer's home.

Then, for reasons he couldn't fathom at the time, one book on Eric's bookshelf had drawn his eye. The title of that book seemed now to take on a new and poignant significance: *The Lord Will Guide You Forever.* If it were not for that book, he would never have discovered the printed email inside it, with correspondence from Degner to Eric. Consequently, he wouldn't have known to search Degner's suite at the Baroque Haven and discover the identity of the private investigator whom Degner had hired, Mickey

Chambers. Subsequently, he would never have met Father Briggs, who would lead him to Daniel Serk. None of it would have happened.

Stockton now believed that the Lord had meant for him to notice that particular book at that particular moment. A Christian book, which Eric himself had written, no less. The discovery of a single book on a bookshelf, set in motion a series of events that led Stockton to the AI node in Poland and brought him face-to-face with the Singularitas cult, Satan and Jesus Christ. As he cruised the darkened highway, his gaze lost in the taillights of Serk's pickup truck, he became increasingly convinced of the comforting notion that none of it had been a mere coincidence.

IT HAD TAKEN Stockton and Serk no more than twenty minutes to construct a simple pyre using some old wooden pallets piled together in one of the fields north of the farmhouse. They positioned the android body on top and doused it in gasoline before lighting a match and setting it all on fire.

In the morning, Serk would bury the remaining debris, safe in the knowledge that none of the hardware would ever be useable again.

It was now 2:30 a.m., and the three of them took a

viewing position about seventy yards from the smoldering conflagration. It was a sufficient distance away so that they wouldn't breathe in the toxic fumes from the plastics and other nasty materials within the dead machine.

Stockton stood behind Zara, cradling her closely, their hands resting together on her belly. Her head snugly fit just beneath his chin, his suit jacket draped over her shoulders, protecting her from the slightly chilly night air.

"It's like we're having a funeral for an old friend," she lamented.

"It does, doesn't it?" Stockton replied, smiling. "Wherever Angel Gabriel's soul is now, he's off to a new parish, just not one from this plane of existence. Like he said, he goes where the good Lord sends him."

Serk maintained his focus on the fire and asked, "What do you think happened to the consciousness of the AI? Did it really have a soul? I wonder where it went to after Gabriel's spirit replaced it."

"I suppose we'll never know," Stockton smiled thoughtfully. "Maybe it truly did become more than a machine. I think, in the end, all it wanted was to be forgiven. Its prayers to Heaven were like an act of contrition."

"You're saying it was confessing its sins to God?"

"I don't know if God forgave the AI for all it had

done, but the first step towards redemption is admitting our failings and mistakes and taking accountability. After that, we repent."

Stockton's stomach knotted with another familiar tug of remorse. "I think that's the reason I've been so angry for so long. I wanted to know why God allowed a situation to arise where I was forced to do what I did during the war. Why did he allow it so that I had to make those choices? Why did I have to choose who lived and who died?"

He wistfully stared into the curls of smoke as they rose skyward. "I've spent all these years living with it and carrying guilt. But the only way to let go of that pain is to be forgiven. I guess the AI figured that out for itself."

He turned to face Zara. "I think I'm ready to talk to Father Philips after all and make a confession."

Zara squeezed his hands in hers and tilted her head slightly. The intoxicating floral fragrance from her hair filled his nostrils. "I'll take you to see him," she smiled with some relief.

Stockton glanced at Serk. "You know, Daniel, you were right from the start. Through some bizarre twist of fate, we got caught up in a battle between Heaven and Hell."

Serk listened intently; his eyes were lost in the flames.

"When we were in Poland," Stockton continued.

"I felt totally powerless when Satan appeared. There was never anything we could do to stop him. It's not Man's place to fight God's battles, only our choice to have faith that he'll save us in the end. It's easy to feel insignificant and helpless when the world seems so dark. But the light is always just about to break on the horizon if you have the courage to believe. I get that now."

"Told ya," Serk grinned.

"Abigail would be proud of you."

The young man's eyes wistfully gleamed, but he didn't reply.

They silently watched the flames for several moments, the only significant source of light in a moonless sky.

"So, New Zealand then?" Stockton asked, breaking the ice.

"Maybe for the honeymoon," Zara cooed.

A playful smirk slowly curled his mouth.

"And it's still a definite no on the Elvis wedding?"

"No!" She giggled.

"Is that a no to the no, which would actually mean yes or just no to the Elvis wedding?"

She swung around to him, chuckling gleefully with doting eyes. "Yes!"

"Okay, I'm really confused now. Maybe we

should just go with the Elvis impersonator to be safe." He grinned mischievously.

Zara threw her head back and guffawed loudly.

An embarrassed-looking Serk distracted himself by kicking a pebble on the ground.

She placed her hands on Stockton's chest and leaned closer to him. "That's a negative on The King at our wedding, soldier." She made a mock salute with her right hand. "We're going with a traditional church wedding, thank you very much."

"Fair enough, Zara. You win this time," he playfully conceded. He turned to Serk. "Consider yourself invited, Daniel, we'd love to have you."

"Yeah, please come," Zara added.

The young man sheepishly smiled, shuffling his feet nervously. "Uh-huh. That'd be cool, thank you."

Stockton said to him, "I'm lucky to have met some really good people during this case. I'd be proud to call you a friend."

Serk smiled and nodded in his usual, overly enthusiastic manner. "Same."

"He's not the only new friend you made," Zara interjected. "The man upstairs is the best friend you could ever have."

The flames of the fire danced hypnotically within his gaze as Stockton remembered what Jesus had said to him.

He repeated the words aloud. "There, in the soil of your doubt, I shall plant my seed of faith."

"What's that old proverb?" asked Zara. "The deeper the roots, the stronger the tree?"

"I think so," Stockton smiled, feeling a new spiritual conviction taking root within him. "I look forward to watching it grow."

AFTERWORD

I'd like to thank you for taking the time to finish reading my first novel. I truly hope you enjoyed reading it as much as I did writing it.

As an independent author, I need your help to promote my work. I'd really appreciate it if you could leave a review of *Deus v Machina* online and tell your friends and family about this book.

Please follow me at the links below:

Subscribe on YouTube.com/@TheDaveCullenShow
Website: https://www.thedavecullenshow.com

Best wishes to you.
Dave Cullen

ABOUT THE AUTHOR

Dave Cullen is an Irish journalist, author, and film critic. He is best known for his pop culture analysis and film and television reviews on his YouTube channel: The Dave Cullen Show.

▶ youtube.com/@TheDaveCullenShow

Printed in Great Britain
by Amazon